T0090290

VUEX

Iris Shephardt

Order this book online at www.trafford.com
or email orders@trafford.com

Most Trafford titles are also available at major online book retailers.

Printed in the United States of America.

ISBN: 978-1-4269-3866-5 (sc)
ISBN: 978-1-4269-3867-2 (hc)

Library of Congress Control Number: 2010910228

*Our mission is to efficiently provide the world's finest, most comprehensive book publishing
service, enabling every author to experience success. To find out how to publish your book, your
way, and have it available worldwide, visit us online at www.trafford.com*

Trafford rev. 08/16/2010

Trafford
PUBLISHING®   www.trafford.com

North America & international
toll-free: 1 888 232 4444 (USA & Canada)
phone: 250 383 6864 ♦ fax: 812 355 4082

CHAPTER 1

THE AIR IS CRISP, with the smell of chocolate-chip cookies fresh from the oven. The sun is shining high in the sky, and people are out and about, shopping in their winter attire. Down the street from the shopping area is a housing district located in West Central Illinois. The houses are a little bit older but are kept in top condition and look inviting to people who drive by them. One house in particular is a spacious three story with brick and woodwork on the outside. There are bushes and evergreens that surround it. On the main floor there's a big living room with family pictures on the walls and various pieces of artwork. There are two sofas, a day bed, a recliner, and three different-sized tables in dark wood in the living area with an old fireplace that is well kept in its original shape. The dining room has a long wooden table covered with an embroidered cloth and surrounded by chairs. The cloth makes the room look elegant and inviting, and candles and flowers are arranged in the center. The kitchen is neat and clean. There are some machines sitting out for immediate use and a small counter for food preparation. The kitchen looks very warm, with various pictures and sheer lace curtains covering the windows. On the stove sits a cookie sheet where the fresh-baked cookies are cooling.

There are three bathrooms in the old house. One is huge and is located upstairs connected to the master bedroom and the hallway. It has an above-average-sized bathtub with jets. The tub has a strange shape that has to be vintage. There are nice shoulders to place things on and a beautiful rug that leads up to the tub. The other bathrooms are the average type found in almost every home.

There are some side rooms in this house, but one in particular has outfits in glass cases up against the wall that look like they're on display. Some are sparkly and glamorous, while others are more rugged with leather embellishments. Altogether they look like something a performer would wear. Placed up against the glass displays are different guitars on stands, including electric, acoustic, and bass. In the living room a woman sits on the sofa with an acoustic guitar on her lap. She is of average size, has blonde hair, and semi-attractive. She is wearing a cold shoulder sweater and relaxed pants. When a chord plays and sounds satisfying to her ears an expression of bliss illuminates the room. She has a perfectionist personality but an open and very strong mind. She isn't afraid to take charge but has a very sensitive nature that she tries not to let show much. To her it's a weakness that can make or break you. She has rare and unusual qualities that make her an appealing and very interesting person, to say the least. Currently, she is experimenting with different sounds to find the right rhythm. Sheet music surrounds her, and it's obvious from the eraser marks that a new song is being written. She keeps striking chords and trying to feel the element and harmony with the song. She tries different sounds and various ways of striking the chords. But then her frustration begins to build, for all of a sudden each time she strikes a chord, she hears the loud noise of something heavy sliding across the floor in the room above her. It finally becomes so frustrating that she puts the guitar down and gets up and approaches the stairs.

"Amber! Amber!!" she calls, getting no answer.

This just adds to her frustration, so up the stairs she goes. There are four rooms and two bathrooms upstairs. The hardwood floor in the hallway is partially covered with a beautiful imported rug. The woman goes to a room at the end of the hallway, where she finds another woman sliding a large cedar chest to the center of the room. She has long dark blonde hair and is wearing a pair of jeans with an off the shoulder sweater. After sliding it one more time, the woman opens the chest and starts taking items out. She places the items all over the floor as though to be sorted. Then, she picks up a booklet that suddenly interests her. So, she closes the chest and sits down on it and begins reading.

"What are you doing?" she asks.

Amber is in deep thought and jumps. The two sisters are opposite in some ways but yet are very close. They have a bond that no one can break.

"Hey, sis, what's up?" Amber asks.

"I'm trying to work on the next album and prepare for our upcoming concert. A better question is what are you doing?" she asks.

"Omani, you've got to see this stuff," Amber states.

"What stuff?" Omani asks.

"You remember the chest Grandma gave us? She told us not to open it until we were at least thirty-five, because that's when the 'changes' would begin. Remember? But I couldn't wait. Besides, it's only three years away for me and one for you. Oh, and look; I found the amber necklace she gave me. It sure has a different look to it. Anyway, I'm never taking it off," Amber replies, putting the necklace on.

"It's a nice necklace. But you know she probably just told us not to open it until a certain age just in case we ran across something only for adults, if you know what I mean," Omani says, laughing.

"Seriously, you've got to check this stuff out. Plus I found these," Amber says.

"What is that?" Omani asks, entering the room to get a closer look. There on the floor in a special bag are two L-shaped rods.

"Well, I was reading this sheet. They're called dowsing rods. I guess Grandma was psychic. Not only that, but here's a diary about how she came into her supposed 'powers.'" Amber begins to explain.

Omani steps back, obviously suspicious of it all.

"And you believe this stuff?" Omani asks.

"Amber, when did Grandma ever lie to us?" Amber states.

Omani comes back into the room and sits down, staring at a picture of Grandma.

"I know. I really miss her," Omani says.

"So do I," Amber says.

"But why keep this all secret? And why after age thirty-five? Why not before?" Omani asks.

"Here—it says in this journal she wrote. It's a birthright handed down through the generations to the women of the family. 'Sparks will fly as you set those free and close the door from the enemy.' Okay, does anybody know what this means? Wow!" Amber says.

"So we're both going to get this?" Omani asks.

"Yep. And check this out. It's a picture of some different cemeteries and other strange places," Amber states.

"No wonder Dad didn't want us around Grandma too much. He wouldn't let Mom talk too much about family history either. Remember? It's all starting to add up. And you know what? I tend to agree with him. I mean, come on, Amber," Omani starts to say.

"What was that?" Amber asks, hearing a noise. It almost sounds like knocking.

"Jim. He said he'd be over after dropping off his brother so we can work on the album for the record company agents. So can you wrap this up and come help us. You're in the band too," Omani says, heading out of the room.

"I'll be right there," Amber says, engrossed in the journal.

Omani shakes her head and goes downstairs and sees Jim taking off his black leather jacket. He hears her and turns around with a big smile on his face.

"Hey, how's my favorite girl?" he says, grabbing her for a quick kiss. He's dressed in a black t-shirt and tight jeans. He's been with the band for three years and dating Omani for about twenty-one months. "Fine, but I think it'll be just you and me working on the album today," Omani says.

"Why? Is Amber sick?" Jim asks.

"No. She found something Grandma left for us. Apparently we're psychic, with some sort of powers. Anyway, enough of that; let's get started," Omani says, reaching for her guitar.

"Seriously? How cool," Jim replies, intrigued.

"You too? Come on; we've got a concert coming up," Omani says, setting the guitar in her lap.

"Come on. I think being psychic would be great. Count me in if it's true," he says.

"Sorry I told you. Here, let's get started. Oh, and by the way, I put together our outfits. I'll show you after we get this song figured out," Omani says.

They start playing, and the rhythm is quickly worked out. They both stand up and start rocking. Omani has her eyes closed, lost in the music. Suddenly she realizes that only her guitar is playing, so she stops and looks around and sees Amber standing there playing with the dowsing rods. She is walking slowly and carefully around the house and is currently in the living room. Jim is totally engrossed in what she's doing. Omani puts her guitar down, glaring at Amber with intense emotion.

"What are you doing?" Omani asks.

"Did you see that?" Amber says with excitement as the rods cross, obviously not paying attention to Omani.

"Yo Amber!!" Omani says, still getting no response. She approaches Amber, and the rods go crazy in every direction. Jim steps back slightly, taken aback by the activity. Omani quickly grabs the rods out of Amber's hands.

"Hey, I was really picking up something," Amber says.

"What's gotten into you? This is so silly and ridiculous! Now come on. We have a concert to prepare for. The rest of the band will be here shortly," Omani says, taking the rods and tossing them in the nearest garbage can.

"Testy, aren't we?" Amber says.

"Excuse me? Who is trying to prepare for a concert here? Plus, this could be our big break. Remember, a few agents are coming. I really want to wow these people. We've worked very hard to get to this point. I'm not going to let some stupid rods get in the way of it. We can go through Grandma's stuff later, but right now we need to get focused. So yeah, I guess I'm a little testy," Omani says as the doorbell rings.

Amber looks at Jim, who just shrugs his shoulders. He seems like the type who just goes wherever the wind blows. He has semi-long hair and tries to look tough, even though his build doesn't reflect it. Amber is very tuned into music but has always had an interest in mystical studies. She has all kinds of books on the subject in her bedroom. She always listened to Grandma's stories, especially the one about how the lives of all the women in the family change forever when they hit a certain age. And always the story stops abruptly, leaving a person hanging to figure out the riddle for themselves.

Amber finds the rest of the band members, Trent and Gabe, at the door. Both of them have been with the band for the entire ten years. Trent and Omani dated for about three years, but it didn't work out. He still has feelings for her but tries to keep it professional. He accepts Jim and Omani are exclusive but silently hopes one day for another chance. Gabe has been dating Cheryl for a little over eight years. He likes to keep his life and relationship very low profile. Amber is the only band member that is married and has been for five years. Trent and Gabe are good friends and make their way into the house with their travel type of musical equipment.

"Hey, everyone, I'm so excited!! Jim and I came up with some serious rocking tunes. Come on, Amber. Get away from the wastebasket and let's get started," Omani says.

"Hey, Amber, I didn't know you were the kid," Gabe said wearing a partially buttoned flannel shirt and jeans. He is medium height with semi-short, brown hair.

"Don't get me started," Omani says.

They all take their places, and Amber leaves the rods in the wastebasket. Jim and Omani play their tunes and impress everyone in the room. Amber picks up her guitar and chimes right in and makes the sound even more memorable.

"These people are going to be so shocked; they won't know what hit them," the drummer, Trent, says wearing two different color t-shirts, black jeans, and a ball cap. He is tall and thin with black hair down to his shoulders.

After hours of playing, everybody starts to yawn and the tunes begin to lose their intensity.

"Hey, why don't we call it a wrap till next time?" Trent says.

"Yeah, hey, can we practice in the place where the concert will be held?" Amber asks.

"Great idea. I'll check on it," Jim says.

"Thanks everybody; till next time," Omani says.

Everybody packs up their stuff and heads for the door while talking among themselves. Jim steps away for a second and walks to the room where all the outfits are. Omani is in there looking everything over. He slides up behind her, wrapping his hands around her waist and kissing the back of her neck.

"Hey," Omani says, turning toward him.

"Hey," he says back in a seducing way.

"Do you think this will really happen?" Omani asks, breaking away and looking all the outfits over.

"Don't you?" he asks, puzzled.

"You know, there just comes a time when you want something so badly that you're just afraid something is going to come and take it away. It's almost like wanting it too much, if there is such a thing. We've been at this for almost ten years. If this doesn't happen, then I guess we'll have to find a real job like my dad always says. I guess I'm just preparing myself for the worst. Otherwise I don't know if I can handle it," Omani says, almost in tears.

"Hey, you're reading too much into this. I've seen bands that play awful and get signed. We'll get it, baby. Especially with you. You're the one who keeps us on task. I think we should sleep on it. I know something that might take your mind off it," he says, whispering in her ear and slowly feeling her waist.

Omani slips away.

"Not tonight. I think I would just be a bore for you. I think I just want to be alone. But thanks. Besides, I think we all need our sleep. We can't afford to miss a beat," Omani states.

"There you go again; always right. I'll see you later," Jim says, walking toward the door.

As he leaves, Omani stands there staring at the outfits. She stares so long it's like they blend together to make one outfit. Finally, she sighs and walks toward the stairs. The dowsing rods are still in the garbage can. Omani shakes her head and continues upstairs. Amber is sitting on the edge of the bed, in her nightgown, hanging up the telephone after a call with her husband. The door is half open. Omani walks past, halfway looking in.

"Good night, Omani," Amber says.

"Good night," Omani replies with a slight depressed voice.

As Omani enters her bedroom she hears the sound of scuffling feet.

"Why did you do that?" Amber asks, standing outside her door and hanging onto the panel.

"Do what?" Omani responds, not turning around.

"Embarrass me like that," Amber says.

Omani turns around, wondering why the subject was even brought up. It's like beating a dead horse, but the horse keeps getting back up.

"Embarrass you?" Omani asks.

"Yeah. I just got off the phone with my husband, and he said—" she starts to say but is interrupted.

"You talked to Kyle about this? Why?" Omani asks, getting upset all over again.

"Because he has a right to know about all of this too. Why are you being so disrespectful to me and Grandma?" Amber asks, stepping out into the hallway and standing firmly as though ready for a lunging fight.

"*Amber!* Look, I'm glad you found that stuff, but you picked the wrong day for it. You knew there was going to be rehearsal. We've worked so hard for this, and I feel like you were just ready to throw it away on some stupid thing we're supposed to have inherited," Omani says.

"*Stupid?* You think the legacy Grandma left us was stupid?" Amber replies, about ready to boil over.

"I don't want to talk about this right now. I'm going to bed," Omani says.

"*Well I do!!* Why are you such a bitch sometimes?" Amber replies. "I do want this band to make it just as much as you do. But this was a big discovery, and you had no respect for it," Amber replies.

Omani takes one hand and slightly hits the wall and with the other hits her thigh. She knows Amber isn't going to drop this, so it's time for a harsh reality check.

"Look, this thing that we supposedly inherited; where is it? And why didn't Grandma ever talk about it? Plus, why didn't she show any signs of having these gifts? And finally, why doesn't anybody else know about it?!! I see it as Grandma's way of giving us some hope, which I dearly love. You know, it's like a remembrance, to let us know we're special. But there is no gift, okay?" Omani explains.

"Well, I think there is. And when Kyle comes back from Europe we're going to check into it," Amber says, heading back to her room.

Great, Omani thinks. Through all this pressure with the band now there are new tensions; one with her sister and the other with supposed gifts that were never discussed. The one thing that Omani ponders is was why Amber decided to go into that room today. It hadn't been opened in the whole three months since they got it. Why all this now? But instead of deeply thinking about it, she gets ready for bed.

During the night while both sisters are sleeping soundly, a suspicious noise could be heard from that room with the chest. It's a soft noise that causes no disruption in the sisters' sleep. As the night continues on, a strange violet-blue glow comes from the chest. Full of mystery, the light comes and goes. As the sun comes up the mysterious light begins to fade. After the sun completely rises, the alarm clocks go off and both girls get out of bed and start their normal routine. After getting dressed Omani goes downstairs yawning and opens the front door. There on the doorstep sits their cat and the daily newspaper.

"Jasper! There you are. Come on, kitty," Omani says, picking up the Norwegian Forest cat with a bushy mane and tail, holding it and kissing it. She puts the cat down and proceeds to pick up the paper. Omani goes into the kitchen and starts to grind beans for the coffee maker. While the grinder is working, Amber comes down the stairs yawning and stretching.

"Jasper!" Amber says, grabbing the kitty and holding it tight.

The cat is purring very loudly. Omani comes out of the kitchen with a fresh cup of coffee in one hand and the paper in the other. As she begins to read it something catches her eye. Omani immediately slaps the paper loudly on her lap and then looks at Amber. Jasper has all of Amber's attention.

"Why did you do that?" Omani asks nicely but sternly.

Amber looks up from petting the cat and looks at Omani with a frown.

"Do what?" Amber asks.

Amber notices Omani looking in a certain direction, so she follows her eyes. There on the sofa lie the dowsing rods arranged perfectly as though somebody had put them there.

"I didn't do that," Amber says.

"Well, I know I didn't," Omani says, going over to pick them up again.

There beside them are the pictures of the cemeteries and other mystical looking places.

"Okay, I get it. Look, I promise that after this concert is over I will look over this stuff with you," Omani says.

"I didn't do it," Amber says, almost scared to approach the couch.

By the look on Amber's face, Omani knows that she's telling the truth.

They both just stand there silently, staring at each other. It's a little overwhelming.

"Jim must have done this. He's such a prankster. I'll get him for this. Would you please put these back in the chest? Like I said, I will be happy to look more into this with you after the concert," Omani says. "I'm going to meet up with the band to prepare for tonight. See you there, sis."

Amber goes upstairs with the rods and pictures in her hands. She opens the door to the room and then quickly steps back. Then she enters slowly with her eyes wide open. The chest door is open, and there on the floor are various writings that weren't there before. It is bewildering. The diary is lying on the floor opened as though to a specific page. Amber slowly approaches it and kneels down to take a look. Next to it she sees a special container with weird writing on it. Amber picks it up while getting closer to the diary. The writing is in a disorganized pattern. It states, "Your powers have been inherited. Tonight it shall begin. The Stoney Graveyard must be cleaned. Take your instruments and special powder with you. They will be waiting. If you don't come, they will come to you."

This sends bone-chilling shivers up and down Amber's spine. Her mouth hangs open while her mind goes wild, wondering what she has done. She takes off with the dowsing rods and the specially decorated container.

"*Omani!!*" Amber shouts, terrified.

Chapter 2

The night is crisp and clear with a slight chill in the air. The moon is shining bright, and people are pulling into the nightclub parking lot one after another. The club has a huge bar with stools and an area with tables with chairs around a large stage. Inside, Omani and Amber are on stage organizing the last-minute preparations. The rest of the band members start to walk off stage toward the back area. After a few minutes Omani and Amber go to the back where there is a crowded area with a couple of tables with some lights set on them. On the tables are some makeup and hair products, and there are a couple of mirrors on the wall. One is full-length, and the other is round. An adjustable mirror stands on the table.

"Did you see all the people coming in?" Gabe says.

"Let's just all stay calm," Omani says.

"Yeah. This is a big night, but let's not let it get the best of us," Amber says, swallowing hard.

As she picks up some makeup, her hands begin to tremble. Omani dismisses it as nerves, but Amber can't get what she saw back at the house out of her mind. While they all continue to get ready, Amber is all thumbs. She keeps dropping things and is trying very hard to keep it together. The guys notice and raise their eyebrows but continue getting ready. Omani is combing her hair in a specific style. They are all dressed in jeans with a hip shirt and shoes. Then the manager of the club comes back smiling and laughing and talking on his cell phone.

"I'll call you back. Hey, Amber and Omani, would you come here please?" he says.

The sisters look at each other, dismayed, and get up and walk over to the manager.

"What did you ladies do?" he asks.

"Do?" Amber asks.

"Yeah. I thought there was only going to be one agent out there. Instead, you've got three," he says.

"*Three!*" Omani says, excited and scared all at the same time.

"Omani, we can do this," Amber says. "Look at this way; if one of them doesn't take us the other probably will. So the odds are in our favor."

"There are three agents out there?" Jim says loudly so all the band can hear it.

They all get excited at once.

"Guys, please! We haven't got anything yet. We need to stay focused," Omani says.

"You're on in five," the club manager says, walking back out.

"Hey, everybody, let's come together," Omani states.

They all join in a circle like a huddle, staring at the ground.

"May this night be special and all of our dreams come true," she comments.

They all put their hands together and lift them into the air in unison. They hear the manager on stage doing the introduction, and the band quickly gathers near the entrance.

"Give a big applause for Akklus," he says.

Out comes the band, waving and going to their spots while the crowd claps loudly. The lights on the stage are strong, and Omani squints, trying to see the audience. It takes a few seconds, but then she is able to see. Over to the left three people are not clapping. It's not hard to decipher that they're the agents. Amber and Omani take a deep breath at the same time. Then the band begins to play. The sound is perfect. Omani and Amber start to sing, sounding unbelievable. People in the audience can't take their eyes off of them. The entire band is dressed in striking colors that indicate their personalities and abilities. With the dim light in those clothes, the band is luminescent. This is such a big moment, and everything is going perfectly. The butterflies are starting to build in Omani, who is beginning to worry that it's too perfect. But she quickly distracts herself, getting into the song at hand. After each song, Omani looks inconspicuously at the agents to see their reactions.

One looks disinterested. Another looks like she's doing something on her cell phone. The third person seems to be focused on eating. None of them are looking at the stage. Omani can feel her heart almost fall out of her chest onto the stage. All she can wonder is what's wrong. Amber looks in the same direction as Omani, noticing the agents. It is disheartening, and Amber quickly goes over to Omani and nudges her.

"Just play," Amber replies.

Omani quickly turns to the band, and they all look up.

"Let's play what we practiced. You know, the new song," Omani says, trying to keep their spirits up.

They all nod in agreement. On the count of three the band begins to play what they practiced hard for a couple of weeks. A few seconds after they start the song, the power suddenly goes out. The only sound is the acoustic guitar and Amber with Omani singing. They quickly stop. It is complete darkness, with no street or emergency lights even on. The crowd gets up screaming and trying to feel their way around. Omani just stands there with disappointment on her face. The band is trying to reach out to each other.

"Omani," Amber says.

There is no response. Amber continues to say her name, walking carefully in the dark. She suddenly bumps into Omani, who has tears flowing silently down her face. Amber can tell something is wrong.

"Hey, they heard us play," Amber says, knowing that her sister is crying.

"But they weren't even interested. All this work for nothing," Omani says.

"It isn't for nothing. Besides, you know how agents are. They don't show what they're thinking. I've heard about how they are. Come on," Amber says, trying to be supportive.

The manager comes out to the center of the stage, trying to get people's attention. Nobody is listening, because they're too busy trying to get out. The manager gets his phone out to see the time. But when he flips it open there is nothing; no power at all. He doesn't think anything of it and just continues to try to steer traffic safely with a dim glow stick.

Amber reaches into her pocket and notices the same thing. She puts the phone back and follows the rest of the band. They go outside, and all that is giving light is the moon.

"What happened?" Jim asks.

"I don't know, but it's freaky," Trent says.

"Yeah, the phones don't even work. How bizarre," Gabe states.

"Let's go," Omani says.

They all begin to step outside. The moon is still shining bright; enough that people can see where to go. Omani feels a strange desire to look up and is shocked. A pair of eyes with no face stare at her from a distance. Omani looks around to make sure it's not a shadow, but there's nothing. The eyes seem to look right at her.

"Hey, Jim, do you see that?" she asks.

Jim looks in the same direction.

"See what?" he asks.

"You don't see those eyes?" she asks.

"Ah, no. You feeling okay?" he asks.

"Yeah, I'm fine. It must just be a shadow," she replies.

Amber, Omani, and Jim all get into the same car. The other two band members and their girlfriends get into a different car and try to start their car to drive off. Jim tries two times to start the car and gets nothing. On the third time the car hesitantly starts. He drives off trying to talk about the music they played tonight, but no one seems interested. As the car approaches Stoney Cemetery it suddenly stalls. The steering wheel locks, and Jim has no choice but to pull over to the side of the road.

"Why are we stopping?" Amber asks.

"It isn't me. The car stalled. I'll check it out," Jim says, getting out.

Omani just stares into the darkness, not saying a word.

"Come on, Omani. Don't throw in the towel now," Amber says.

"I need to take a walk," Omani says, opening the car door and getting out.

Amber opens her car door and gets out too. Quickly Amber realizes where they are. She's gasping for air. Amber turns back around and reaches under the seat and gets the rods and the canister. She holds it close to her body while trying to catch up to Omani. Jim notices them walking toward the cemetery. He puts the hood back down on the car and runs to catch up with the other two.

"I don't know what's wrong with the car. Everything seems to be fine. I'll try it in a little bit. Is she okay?" Jim asks.

"I don't know. Let's just give her some space. I'm going to walk with her. Why don't you just stay a little behind us?" Amber says.

He agrees and stays a few steps behind. Omani keeps looking straight ahead, not really interested in her surroundings. As they continue to walk Jim notices something strange. The further they walk into the cemetery the more he can see blue-violet sparks going back and forth between the two sisters. He starts to think it's a figment of his imagination and shakes his head. When he looks up, it does it again, but this time stronger.

"Guys," Jim says.

Amber looks back with a finger on her lips to indicate to Jim to be quiet. He stays quiet for just a few seconds, until the sparks start to go again.

"Guys!" he says again, but a little more firmly.

Amber turns back again.

"Don't you see it?" he asks in a loud whisper.

Amber frowns. Jim steps back a little bit, not knowing what to think of what he is seeing. The sisters keep walking together in silence, not aware of anything.

"It's just that we worked so hard and now I feel like it was for nothing. Is it the hair? The face? What? Why didn't they like us?" Omani says, staring at the ground.

Amber grabs Omani by the arm to stop her. Then she grabs Omani's face and looks directly into her eyes.

"Listen to me. We don't know what they think yet. I think you're settling for the worst-case scenario. Agents are like that. They appear that they don't like you when they really do. It's all part of the game. You remember what happened to Liz, right?" Amber asks.

Suddenly the light goes on for Omani.

"Yeah. You're right. They treated her the same way, and look at her now. Thanks, Amber. I couldn't have asked for a better sister," Omani says, starting to look around suspiciously. "Do you hear that?"

"Yeah, it's like rustling leaves," Amber says.

"But there are no leaves here," Omani says.

The sisters quietly look around. Jim is standing some distance from them with a look of horror on his face.

"Jim, are you okay?" Omani asks.

Jim isn't looking at either sister. Instead he seems to be looking past them as though his sight is fixed on something else. He starts to gasp, trying to say something, but no words come out. Finally, he resorts to lifting his right hand to a ninety-degree angle and pointing past the sisters.

"Jim?" Omani asks, concerned.

He gasps louder.

"*What is that?*" he exclaims.

Amber and Omani quickly turn around and see something terrifying—about eight dark stick-looking figures walking toward them in a zigzag manner. There are no faces or arms or legs. It's just dark figures that are very tall but only a few inches wide.

"Omani! I think they're coming this way," Amber states.

"*Run!*" Omani says.

They all take off running toward the entrance where the car is parked.

All three are running at top speed. While running Amber trips over a small grave marker and lands face down. Omani notices that Amber is not beside her and stops.

"*Amber!! Amber!!*" Omani says.

"Ow!!" Amber says, trying to get up.

"Jim, Amber is hurt!! *Jim!!*" Omani says, trying to get his attention.

He keeps running. Omani turns around to go back for Amber.

"*Come on! Get up!*" Omani exclaims.

It suddenly becomes deathly quiet.

"They're gone," Amber says, getting up.

Omani looks around, feeling strange.

"No, they're not. They're surrounding us," Omani says, seeing the dark figures zigzagging while standing still.

"What do they want?" Amber asks.

"I don't know, but they're getting closer," Omani says.

Amber looks down and sees the canister and the dowsing rods on the ground. She quickly picks up the canister so fast that its top comes off. Then some strange dust comes out of it and goes up the air rather than falling to the ground. Amber can't take her eyes off of it. Suddenly a large oval-shaped light appears. While Amber is staring at the light the dowsing rods start to go crazy in Amber's hands.

"Omani," Amber says, trying to get her attention quietly.

"They're backing away," Omani says.

"I think I know why. Look!" Amber says.

Omani turns around and sees the large oval light.

"Where did that come from?" Omani asks.

"From this canister of Grandma's," Amber says, "Check out these rods. They're going crazy."

Amber turns toward the dark figures, and suddenly the rods become erect toward them.

"What are you doing?" Omani asks.

"Nothing. The rods are doing this," Amber replies.

The dark figures stop. The sisters don't know what to think. Then the rods start acting funny.

"They're tingling in my hand. It almost hurts," Amber says.

"Drop them," Omani says.

Amber tries to let them go out of her hand. "I can't," she says, scared.

Omani grabs hold of the rods, and suddenly the dark figures come racing toward them. Both ladies scream. Jim is standing beside the car hearing the screams and trembling. Both sisters close their eyes, thinking it's doomsday. A wind picks up from out of nowhere. The electricity is strong as they can feel the things whip past them. While all this is occurring, Omani opens her eyes. She sees the dark figures going into the light. When the last one goes through, the winds stop and the bright oval light slowly disappears.

"What was that?" Amber asks.

"I don't know, but I think it's time to find out the so-called gifts Grandma gave us. Come on; let's go before those things come back," Omani says.

The sisters run to the car. Omani's look of fear turns to rage as she approaches Jim.

"*Where were you??!!!!!* We almost got killed!" Omani asks in his face.

"I wasn't sticking around for those things, whatever they are. They weren't coming up to say hello. And you, who in the hell are you people?" he asks.

"Who are we? What about you? You're the one who left us!" Omani asks.

"That … that … blue glow. What the hell happened? What *were* those things? Better yet, don't tell me. I just want to go home," Jim says, almost in tears and shaking in his shoes.

"Fine! Be a coward! You know you always wanted to experience something supernatural. You do, and what happens—you run!" Omani says, looking for some type of response. Jim just stands there trembling and looking away.

"Give me the keys," Omani states, glaring at Jim.

The keys are loosely hanging on by a finger on his hand. She reaches over and grabs them, and Amber and Omani get into the car. As it starts up the local power comes back on. Omani is getting ready to put the car in gear but then looks out the driver's window. There stands Jim out by the side of the road.

"What are you doing? Get in," Omani says.

Jim looks toward Omani and Amber but doesn't respond. Instead he steps back a few more paces. Then out of the blue a cab pulls up beside Jim.

"You're kidding me! We almost die and you called a cab!! Jerk!!" Omani says.

"More like asshole!" Amber states.

Omani puts the car in gear and speeds off into the night. Neither sister has a clue to what awaits them. But they will soon find out that their lives have changed forever.

CHAPTER 3

THE NEXT MORNING THE sun is shining in the house, which is quiet except for one room where there are shuffling noises and thud sounds. It's Omani and Amber going through the cedar chest their grandmother left. Both ladies are still in their nightgowns with coffee cups sitting on a small table. They're placing items all over the floor as though sorting them. Each item taken out of the chest is carefully looked over and then placed somewhere strategic. Omani stands up, scratching her head and trying to organize everything in her mind. Amber just keeps pulling more items out.

"Well, this is the last item," Amber says, placing it on the floor, not realizing that there at the base of the chest are more items hidden from view.

Omani is still standing in the same spot scratching her head.

"There's stuff here that I've never seen before. If we inherited whatever it is wouldn't we know what this stuff is?" Omani asks.

"Not necessarily. That's why Grandma left this book," Amber states.

"What book?" Omani asks, looking around for it.

Amber picks it up from behind her and gives it to Omani. The book cover is of rippled leather. It has obviously been used a lot in the past. Omani opens the book, and some papers fall out onto the floor. She kneels down to pick them up and sees a picture of a form that looks like the dark figures from the night before.

"Amber, check this out. Remind you of anything?" Omani says, holding up the sheet.

"Those things!!" Amber says, getting up instantly, not able to take her eyes of the paper.

"Yeah, apparently according to Grandma they're demons looking for souls," Omani states, reading in bewilderment.

"So why did they come after us?" Amber asks.

"Good question. Hey, what is that?" Omani asks, pointing to a large canister with writing and strange designs on it in various colors.

"It's like the one from last night but bigger," Amber states, looking it over.

"What's in it?" Omani asks.

Amber carefully opens the canister and then looks inside.

"Looks like a sparkly powder," Amber says.

"Okay, before we open anything else, I think we need to read everything Grandma wrote. So let's get all the writings and take them downstairs. All this stuff may be neat, but we need to be careful. We don't know what we're getting ourselves into yet, especially after last night. Oh, if we could only talk to Grandma about this before she suddenly passed away three months ago," Omani states.

Amber gathers all the documents and places them in a pile. Then they each pick up part of the pile.

"Is that your phone ringing?" Amber asks.

"Yeah. I'll meet you downstairs," Omani says, holding some documents in her hands and leaving the room.

Omani quickly goes into her bedroom and opens her purse, scrambling about and searching for the phone. She pulls it out with the ring even louder.

"Hello," Omani says. "This is she."

Meanwhile, Amber takes the articles downstairs and sits at the dining table spreading out the documents in order to read them. She picks up one document and starts reading. Suddenly Amber hears her sister running down the stairs.

"Amber, it was one of the agents. You were right. They liked us," Omani says, jumping up and down with excitement.

"*Yes!!* See, I told you," Amber says.

"And they said that it was unfortunate that the power went out and they would like to hear us again. We get a second chance! This is great!!!" Omani says, screaming with excitement.

Amber gets up and starts jumping up and down. This is huge for these girls, and they're not taking it lightly. While they are jumping up and down the phone rings again. Omani quickly stops jumping to get her composure.

"Maybe it's another agent! Or maybe they just decided to sign us now!" Omani says without looking at the number on the front of the phone.

"Hello," she says.

Amber has a huge smile on her face waiting with anticipation. Omani's joyous moment quickly turns to concern. She sits down, listening and drooping over in silent pain. Amber knows that whatever it is isn't good. She watches the expressions on Omani's face very closely. After another minute, Omani hangs up the phone and drops it beside her on the floor. She places her head in her hands, staring at the floor while tears drip from her eyes silently.

"What's wrong?" Amber asks cautiously.

Omani slowly looks up, wiping tears away.

"It was Trent. He says that Jim dropped out of the band. Plus he left town this morning and won't be coming back. He didn't even say good-bye," Omani says, staring into space. Amber stops what she's doing and rushes to her sister's side.

"Omani, I'm sorry," Amber says, trying to figure out how to comfort her sister.

Omani rocks back and forth in the chair slowly while in shock and disbelief.

"You know we were together for two years. Apparently it meant nothing. You know how guys and I go. This just proves it," Omani says.

"Yeah, but he was a coward. There will be someone for you," Amber says.

"Listen to you. You're the married one. You never had trouble getting a man even without trying. I can't even get a man to look at me with a two-foot pole. That's what it seems like anyway. And when I do, he turns out to be a flake. Why can't I have something real? What's wrong with me?" Omani asks.

"Nothing. You just haven't met the right one yet," Amber says.

"Have you ever thought that maybe there isn't one? I mean, look at my history. I think I just need to accept that there's no one and that I will never marry. It's been nothing but strife for me anyway," Omani says.

"There will be someone. You're just trying to force it. Besides, shouldn't we be focusing on getting a record deal with one of these agents?" Amber says.

Omani instantly stands up, horrified.

"*Oh my God!! The band!!* What are we going to do without Jim? *Shit!* This isn't happening," Omani says, walking in circles, sighing.

"We'll just have to find another guitarist," Amber says.

"Now? How are we going to do that, Miss Optimistic? These agents aren't going to understand. Where are we going to find someone that good and fast?" Omani asks, all stirred up.

"I'll place an article in the paper today. Look, we'll get someone. Omani, we will do this. Look at me," Amber says, placing her hands on her sister's shoulders to get her attention and focus. Omani is looking away, all upset.

Omani takes a few deep breaths, trying to calm down. Then she looks at Amber and gives her a sad smile and walks up to the window and stares outside, gathering herself. After a few minutes, she turns around and faces Amber.

"You're right. I need to think positive. The agent says we can set the date. So we have a little time. You think someone will respond to the paper?" Omani asks.

"Only one way to find out. How about you just focus on figuring out Grandma's documents and I'll work on the ad," Amber replies.

They sit down at the table. Amber starts writing up something for the paper while Omani starts carefully looking through the papers. Although broken-hearted, Omani soon stops thinking about Jim and becomes engrossed in the documents. The various pictures are mesmerizing. Then the phone rings loudly again, but she doesn't even hear it. Amber starts to get annoyed by the ring and gets ready to say something, but then it stops.

"Hey, take a look at this," Omani says.

She lays out the documents on the table so Amber can see.

"What is it?" Amber asks, looking at the documents.

"Well, piecing this together it looks like this has been going on for generations. There's a list of people on this sheet," Omani says, looking it all over.

"Aunt Kara? Who would have ever thought?" Amber says, stunned.

"Yeah, and look at the other family members from the past," Omani says.

Amber pulls up a chair closer to her sister and starts reading the other documents lying there. Omani just stares at all the family names, stunned.

"Look, here's a list about inheriting powers," Amber says.

"Powers?" Omani asks, setting a document aside to look at the one Amber is holding. The document is crumpled, as though it was supposed to have been thrown away years ago.

"Yeah. It doesn't state what they are, just that we will come into them. Then there's this," Amber says, showing the bottom of the crumpled paper.

"There's another one of us? What does that mean? We're the only sisters, aren't we?" Omani asks.

"According to all of this, it's someone not related to us. It's the one who can see safely past all gates. Whatever that means," Amber says, feeling puzzled.

Something suddenly clicks in Omani, like a light bulb coming on.

"Did you see those eyes last night when we left the club?" Omani asks.

"No. What eyes?" Amber asks.

"So you didn't see anything?" Omani asks.

"*No.* What did they look like?" Amber asks.

"They were red and looked angry. There was no face, but the eyes were huge. There's no way you can have missed them if you could see them. So maybe it's me that this document is referring to," Omani says.

"It can't be," Amber replies.

"Why?" Omani states.

"Because it says right here that it's not of blood. And it says for the powers to work properly this person has to be a part of it," Amber says.

"Well then, who in the hell is it? Nobody else saw those eyes last night. Based on everything, it's got to be a woman. I know; maybe it's one of those agents. One of them did act suspicious," Omani replies.

"Could be. At this point we don't know. Check this out," Amber says, holding a document that appears to have a riddle component to it.

It says, "For every entry point is an exit, and the guardians hold the key. There will be one who unleashes the great entity. The guardians must unite and combine souls, for it will take all and its powers to fight it. The guardians must strengthen their powers, for their weaknesses are known. Each has a gift, and the light reflects it. Be forewarned that if you choose not to strengthen the powers they will be taken along with their soul. They will come for you, and there is no hiding place. Prepare, for the battle awaits."

That is the end of that particular document. On the side are descriptive drawings of a couple of rickety-looking houses, various landmarks with no descriptions, and the mention of those cemeteries along with other places.

"Are we witches?" Amber asks with a look of fear.

"I don't think so. This is very specific stuff. It's like we're some sort of guardians to the other side or something. I think we protect souls from demonic forces for both the living and the dead. And without us the world would be in a spiritual anarchy," Omani says.

"So then what are our powers?" Amber asks.

"Good question. It doesn't say anywhere. And who is this other person? One riddle after another. You know Grandma never talked in riddles. This is weird."

They both ponder the documents. It is all mind-boggling. Omani looks over the same documents again to make sure she didn't miss something. Meanwhile, Amber picks up the divining rods and starts walking around the room behind Omani. At first the rods do nothing and remain neutral. Amber frowns a little. There is a picture that shows that they cross when around a presence or some type of energy. Amber walks around the living room. As she takes slow steps the rods begin to move very slowly. She stops to see what happens. They go neutral again, so she takes another step. The rods begin to move again. They seem to begin to point to the right. So she turns right a little and takes another step. The rods begin to move quickly. Then they cross and stop. Amber looks around and doesn't see anything suspicious. She takes another step. The rods open and move. Then they come together again.

"Hey, Omani, look at this," Amber says.

Omani turns around and sees the rods crossed. Her mouth opens slightly. She slowly gets up, uncertain of what to think.

"What does that mean?" Omani asks.

"According to this it either means we found water, an electrical line, or a spirit. I don't see any sinks or faucets nearby, and there's no electrical outlet right here. So my guess is that we found a spirit," Amber says.

Omani stands, uncertain what to think or do. She just stares at the rods, which remain crossed. When she takes a small step toward them, they jiggle a little, so she stops.

"If there's someone here that would like to speak to us could you make the rods uncross and cross again?" Omani states, not expecting anything to occur.

They watch the rods closely. Nothing happens.

"There must be an electrical wire under the floor," Omani says.

"Look," Amber says, standing perfectly still.

Omani looks and sees the rods begin to straighten out. Then they cross again and stop just like she asks.

"Okay, that's freaky," Omani says.

"Are you a boy?" Amber asks, to see what happens.

"Amber!!" Omani says, standing back.

The rods uncross and begin to move as though shaking their head no.

"Are you a girl?" Amber asks.

The rods stop and cross.

"Did you just see that?" Amber asks, breathing fast.

"Yeah, but do we know what we're doing?" Omani asks.

Suddenly the doorbell rings. Both ladies scream and jump for a second.

Then there's a knock at the door.

"Who is that?" Amber asks.

"It's probably the band wanting to discuss Jim's wonderful departure. We have to put this stuff away. No one can know about this; at least not right now," Omani says, scrambling and grabbing things and figuring out where to stuff them. There's another knock at the door, this time louder.

"Coming!" Omani says. "Put the stuff somewhere. I'm going to answer the door."

Amber looks around as Omani heads for the door. She sees a seat cushion and lifts it. Then she places the documents there and the rods under the sofa. Omani answers the door; it's the rest of the band. They rush in babbling about their concerns since Jim left.

"What are we going to do?" Trent asks in the uproar.

"Calm down. Amber and I discussed it. She's placing an ad in the paper," Omani says, trying to be positive.

"Oh, that's just great. We're on the verge of possibly getting a contract, after ten hard years, and you're going to put an ad in the paper to see what looney we can attract," Trent says.

"Do you have any other ideas? If so I would love to hear them," Omani says matter-of-factly.

"Well, not off the top of my head. But there has to be a better idea than that. We can be doing auditions for hours when we should be practicing. I'll ask around and see if anybody knows someone. Other than that, are we going to practice today?" Trent asks.

"Umm, yeah. Come on in and we'll go over some stuff," Omani says, giving a stressed look to Amber, who just shrugs her shoulders.

"Hey, Gabe came up with something unique with the keyboard. You've got to hear it," Trent says, sitting down on the chair where the documents are stashed.

"Yeah. I brought my keyboard just in case you want to hear it," Gabe says.

"Okay, do you think Amber and I can get changed really quick before we start?" Omani says.

The guys shrug their shoulders indifferently. It's like they don't even notice the fact that the ladies are still in their nightgowns.

"Great. By the way, did either of you see anything strange last night outside the club before we got into our cars after the power outage?" Omani asks casually.

The guys look at each other and then shake their heads no.

"Well, okay then. Be back in a few," Omani says, going up the stairs with Amber.

"Where did you put the stuff?" Omani asks.

"Don't worry; it's somewhere safe," she replies.

"Let's do our practice then get back to where we left off. Come on," Omani whispers to her sister.

Chapter 4

Three days later Amber is on the computer in one of the side rooms looking up information about guardians. She tries many different words to search and comes up mostly empty. She tries one more attempt under another search word, typing in "guardians" and "dowsing rods." Suddenly something comes up, and it looks like a good article. She clicks on it and waits for the article to open. It turns out to be a couple of pages long. The more she reads, the more her breath is taken away.

Omani opens the front door and throws her car keys onto the small table by the entryway. She quickly takes off her light coat. She can't see Amber yet but knows that she somewhere nearby.

"Did I miss the first guitar audition?" Omani asks, placing her coat in the closet.

There's no response, so Omani walks around, trying to find her sister. She finds her in the side room by the dining area on the computer.

"Hey," Omani says.

"Hey," Amber replies without looking up.

"Did I miss the first audition?" Omani asks.

"No," Amber replies, still not looking up.

"Wow, looks like you found something engrossing," Omani says.

"I think I found a clue about being a guardian," Amber says, printing the article.

Omani hears the printer going off and goes over to it. She picks up the couple of pages and starts to read the article.

"We're suppose to spiritually clean houses and rid places that opened up a portal through to the occult. These are people who dabble in the occult not realizing what they are doing. The problem is once you open the portal, it must be closed. If not, these things come through, creating havoc," Amber says.

Omani's jaw drops as she reads the article. She can't take her eyes off it, reading it all the way through. When she gets to the end she encounters a surprise.

"Did you read the last part of this article?" Omani asks.

"Yep. But I have a feeling that we've only scratched the surface," Amber replies, horrified.

"That's us. Oh my God. How are we supposed to do this?" Omani asks, placing the article back on the table.

The last part of the article is facing out and up. It states that a special group of guardians will come to vanquish the great entity. It also states that there is proof that this great entity has already been released through the great portal. It shows the signs of what to look for of the great entity. That part is covered up.

"It's 1:30. That guitarist will be here any minute," Amber says.

"Okay. We'll discuss this later. Right now let's put it away," Omani says as the doorbell rings.

Omani tries to quickly regain her composure and heads for the door. Amber takes the printed article and places it in a folder where they have notes to take from the scheduled auditions. Omani answers the door, and there stands more of child than a man. He has pimples all over his face and looks all of fifteen, if that. The boy stands there with confidence as though expecting a medal.

"Can I help you?" Omani asks.

"Yeah. I'm here for the audition," he says.

Omani looks him over, thinking that maybe Trent was right.

"Oh. Come on in," she says, watching him walk with arrogance.

As he walks in the door, they can hear a person yelling from a car. It looks like his mother. She yells so loudly the whole neighborhood can hear that she will be back in fifteen minutes. She also tells him to not be late. His face turns a little red, and he quickly enters so the door can be closed. As he walks toward the living room, Amber sees him and almost gasps. The sisters look at each other with disapproval as the boy sits down and whips out his guitar.

"How old are you?" Amber boldly asks.

Omani looks at her sister as though almost offended. The boy sits straight up as though honored at the question.

"I'm fourteen. But I'll be fifteen in two months," he says proudly.

"Okay, can you play rock 'n' roll or hip-hop with a country twist?" Omani asks hesitantly.

"Yeah," he says, putting his guitar in his lap and preparing to play.

Before either sister can say anymore, he begins to play. When he first begins it sounds very professional, and the sisters look at each other, shocked. Then after a few minutes, he begins to miss notes but continues to play. It's as though he's hoping the ladies wouldn't notice.

"Thank you," Omani says.

The boy doesn't listen and continues to play.

"You can stop now!" Amber says, trying to get his attention.

He looks up, knowing he messed up. He has a puppy-dog look on his face as though looking for sympathy and perhaps believing that sympathy would keep him in the game.

"Sorry," he says. "Just a little nervous."

"We understand. But look, we need someone who can possibly go on tour. And I would think with your age that you're still in school. So keep practicing, and someday I think you will be ready. But at this time you're not what we're looking for," Omani says, fearing that she will break the boy's heart.

He quickly places his guitar in its case and dashes for the door without looking back.

"Guess he took that well, huh?" Amber says.

"Okay, no more teenagers. You answer the door next," Omani says.

Just after she says that the doorbell rings. Amber gets up and heads for the door. Omani sits there, fearing that it's another kid. But when Amber greets the person she sounds positive. Omani turns around and sees a woman who seems to be around the same age as the sisters. She has long red hair and is of medium build and has an appealing quality to her that radiates throughout the room. The sisters look at each other as though they may have hit the jackpot. Not only that, but they are silently wondering if this is the third guardian.

"Please sit down," Amber says.

"Have you played in a band before?" Omani asks.

The lady sits straight up, brushing her long red hair back with her fingers.

"Yes, thank you. I have worked with various bands. Music is harmony for the soul. Would you like me to play?" she asks.

"Sure. Here. This some of the music we play," Omani says, handing her a sheet.

The lady looks it over and smiles. She picks up her guitar and places it in her lap.

"By the way, my name is Becky." she comments while beginning to play.

As soon as she begins to play, it's like angels chiming. It's wonderful and breathtaking, and the sisters look at each other and nod.

"Thank you, Becky . That was beautiful," Amber comments.

Both sisters smile.

"So, have you ever toured?" Omani asks.

The lady sits back, almost on edge. She scratches her head and appears slightly frustrated. The sisters aren't sure what to make of the strange behavior.

"Well, I have done some research. As I understand you're a local band, right?" she asks.

"Yes, but recently some agents have been observing us. We may get a record deal. If so, it means touring. You sound great. We would love to hear more. You may be a good fit," Omani explains.

Becky takes a few deep breaths and sighs.

"Thanks. But I'm looking to play in a local band. You see, I got married two years ago, and we have a one-year-old son. I don't think my husband would approve. But I thank you," she says, getting up.

The sisters look at each other, disappointed, and follow Becky to the door.

"Sorry. Maybe some other time." Becky says, leaving.

Amber closes the door.

"That may have been our best candidate. This sucks," Omani says.

Before either sister has a chance to sit down again, the doorbell rings.

"Your turn," Amber says.

They both roll their eyes, and Omani slowly lifts her hand to the door knob. She is scared to see what's on the other side. She takes a deep breath and then just opens the door. There stands a very old man with a guitar. He has to be close to seventy, if not older. His hair is all gray. When he smiles it's obvious he has loose dentures, and they are crooked and discolored. The ladies are dumbfounded. The man stands there with his guitar, smiling.

"Hi, uhh. We're sorry; the position has been filled," Omani says and quickly closes the door.

"Did you see that guy?" Amber says, laughing.

"Well, he's got guts. I'm just afraid he would have a heart attack on the road," Omani says.

"Did you see those teeth?" Amber says.

"You answer the next one. I've got to go to the bathroom. Then I think I'll brush my teeth," Omani says.

"Don't forget to floss," Ambers says, laughing.

While Omani is upstairs, Amber looks over some music items. Then the doorbell rings. She gets up, heading for the door while still laughing slightly from the last person.

"This is going to be good. They always come in threes," she says under her breath.

Amber composes herself and then opens the door. There she finds a man with well-styled almost shoulder-length hair. He has on a stylish rocking hat with a bandana, a T-shirt, black leather jacket, steel toe boots, and cut jeans. He stands there with a smirky smile of confidence.

"Come in," Amber says, dazzled by his look.

He takes off his coat and hat. Immediately Amber notices tattoos on his arms. He comes across as tough but yet seems to have gentle side to him. It's obvious that he likes to be his own person.

"You have a lovely home," he says.

"Thanks. But this is my sister's. I'm staying here a little while since my husband is in Europe. How long have you been playing the guitar?" she asks.

"Since I was little," he says.

Amber can't take her eyes off him. There is just something about him. He has a magnetic personality.

"Please come in and sit down," she says.

"I would rather stand, thank you. I play best that way," he says.

Suddenly they hear footsteps. The striking man looks toward the stairs as Omani starts coming down.

"I heard the doorbell ring. Who is—" she begins to say but suddenly stops. She remains on the stairs. The man and she just stare at each other while Amber looks at both of them. She sees that her sister's breath is taken away.

"This must be your sister," he says calmly, still staring.

"This is Omani," Amber says.

"Hi," she says, acting all shy and stunned by the guy.

Amber gives her sister a look to snap her out of it.

"Umm, I take it you're here to audition for the guitarist," Omani says.

"Yep. Got it right here," he says, not able to take his eyes off of Omani.

She keeps looking at him but tries to stay focused.

"Well, okay. Here's a glimpse of our music. Do you think you can play it?" Omani asks with her hands trembling.

He gives a confident smile. He doesn't even study the piece but instead gets out his guitar and prepares to play.

"Better yet, why don't I play and you listen and then tell me what you think. Anybody can play sheet stuff. I want to show you what I can do. I'm quite sure I can satisfy you," he says, winking at Omani.

The sisters are mesmerized by him, but it's obvious that he's interested in Omani. She keeps her composure but on the inside is melting. He begins to play softly, an almost romantic and seductive tune. Then just as the ladies are getting comfortable with the sound, he changes goes into more of a rock 'n' roll mode. He strikes the chords with attitude and emotion. They can feel the intensity without a word being spoken. After a few minutes of rock 'n' roll, he goes back to a soft but aggressive sound. It's captivating. Finally, he plays a note and makes it last as long as possible. Afterward, he stops the sound and then looks up with a smile, shaking his hair back. Both ladies are speechless. He looks at them, waiting for some sort of response. Instead he gets stares.

"So what did you think?" he asks.

"What did you say your name was again?" Omani asks.

"I didn't. But thanks for asking. I'm Bryce," he responds.

"Umm, my sister and I are going to have a talk. We'll be right back," Amber says.

They go into the kitchen area, where there is a sliding door that separates the kitchen from the dining area and living room. Amber pulls it shut. Bryce puts his guitar away and slicks his hair back. Then he begins to wander around the living room.

"Wow! He's good. He's even better than Jim!" Omani says.

"Yeah, but ..." Amber begins to say.

"But what?" Omani asks.

"His look. Do you think he'll fit in?" Amber asks.

"Of course. That's a silly question. I think we should go for it. I don't think we'll get anyone else that good," Omani says.

"I think he might like you," Amber replies.

"Please. You know how men and I go. Besides I'm not ready for any romantic hassles. Come on; he's probably getting suspicious," Omani says.

The sisters go out to the living area. They both notice that he is not in the immediate area and look at each other, hoping he didn't leave. They begin a quick search around the house and then see him by the window in the living room.

"Oh, there you are," Amber says, feeling relieved.

Bryce is holding a picture of their grandmother in his hands. He places it back on the coffee table and then turns around.

"I suppose you had your talk," he comments.

"Yes. Yes we did. How do you feel about traveling and touring?" Omani asks.

He looks her up and down as though he is imagining her naked.

"Great. I like to shake things up a bit," he says.

"Well then, we would like to have you as part of our band," Omani says.

"Then it's settled. When do I meet the rest of the group? Are they as lovely as you two?" he asks.

"Umm, you can meet them tonight. And they're guys. We work together as a group. Plus it's best to keep business and pleasure separated. Listen, sorry to cut this party short, but I need to make a phone call. See you tonight. Here's the address where we will meet," Omani says.

She heads upstairs. Amber gives him a smile, getting ready to guide him to the door. He watches Omani leave the room and then smiles.

"My, she's a best testy, huh?" he says.

"Just got over a bad relationship," she says.

"Is that why the business and pleasure rule?" he asks.

"Umm, I don't think it's for me to discuss. But welcome to the band. I'm looking forward to you meeting the rest of them tonight," Amber says.

"Me too. I'm ready to take the band on a journey they've never been on before. Don't worry; I'll see myself out. Later," Bryce says, going for the door with his guitar. He walks away with a level of confidence rarely seen. It's very appealing and spellbinding, and it's obvious that this man knows himself and his abilities. The winds of change for this group have begun on many levels. The question is are they ready for it?

CHAPTER 5

THAT EVENING GABE AND Trent are in a makeshift recording studio at a friend's house, practicing the drums and the keyboard. The rest of the band hasn't shown up yet. Distracted, Trent hits the drums softly and without a goal. He stares out into space as though in deep thought. Trent misses the drums a few times but doesn't even realize it. Gabe notices but keeps playing. He knows that Trent is the type you don't question. He's found that if a situation is brought up too soon, Trent makes everybody pay for it. He has a vengeful attitude and isn't afraid to use it. Gabe knows that Trent will bring up what's on his mind when he's ready. Finally, Trent stops hitting the drums and turns around to Gabe.

"Do you know this guy they picked?" Trent asks.

"No. Just got a message from Omani that his name is Bryce," Gabe says.

"Me too. Why weren't we in the decision process?" he asks.

"We weren't when Jim was chosen," Gabe says.

"Exactly; that's my point. I know that the two sisters formed the band, but I think we should make decisions together," Trent says.

"I agree. But could you have been there for those auditions? I know I couldn't. If we had to arrange all that around all our schedules, we would be at this for months," Gabe says.

"You're probably right," Trent says.

"But if it's a big concern for you, talk to them about it. You know they're open-minded," Gabe replies.

Just then, a door creaks upstairs, and they know that the rest of the band has arrived. Trent and Gabe prepare themselves to meet the new band member. They both make sure they're in performance position.

The door to the basement opens, and they hear the sounds of shoes hitting the stairs. The sisters are giggling with each other.

"Hey, guys," Amber says when they hit the bottom.

"Hey," Trent and Gabe say in unison.

Omani has a big smile on her face. She looks at Gabe and Trent and then looks toward the top of the stairs. Her hands are in her back pocket.

"I would like to proudly announce the new member of our band. His name is Bryce. Come on down," Omani says.

They hear Bryce's feet lightly hitting the stairs as he comes down. He shakes his hair back and gives a greasy smile as soon as he sees the guys. He waves at Gabe and Trent, uncertain of what to say.

The two men look him over. His unique look takes them off guard. Then they notice the tattoos and see that he's very attractive and appears to take good care of himself. It's difficult to tell his age; he is older than the ladies by at least five years if not more. But his appearance is so striking that nobody cares.

"This is Trent, and this is Gabe. You guys, wait till you hear him play. Come on," Amber says.

"This ought to be good," Trent says sarcastically, looking at Gabe.

Gabe doesn't say anything.

"Come on. Let's play. Bryce had a chance to look over the music already. I want to play a number so you can hear him. Let's play our first musical number from the other night," Omani says with excitement.

Trent rolls his eyes, uncertain of what to think. But he positions himself to play. Gabe, the "go with the flow" guy, smiles and perks up, ready to play. They begin the musical number the same way as usual. When the heart of the song begins, Bryce lets the guitar strings of his Rickenbacker be heard, and the rock star sound ricochets off the walls. The band continues to play, and the ladies sing. When the song is finished everybody stops but Bryce. He plays the two last A and G half notes, which really tie up the song. Amber and Omani are impressed and look at him in awe.

"Where did you come up with that?" Amber asks.

"I played the song alone and thought it needed something a bit more," he replies.

"What? Like your hair?" Trent asks sarcastically.

"So you noticed. Didn't think guys like you recognized style," Bryce replies.

"Style? Hah! Anybody can let their hair grow and hope for the best," Trent smirks.

Omani turns and looks at Trent disapprovingly. He gives Omani a quick smile with a little attitude at the end of it. Amber notices the behavior and wonders if he is truly upset or jealous of what this new guy has done.

"Are you okay?" Amber asks Trent.

"Yeah. Now that we have fancy strings here we can get our contract," he says.

Omani gives a stern look to Trent, noticing the sharp remarks.

"Trent, can I talk to you a minute?" Omani asks.

"Sure. What's up?" he asks.

"Not here. Upstairs," Omani says, looking at him firmly.

He places his drumsticks down and gets up with a cocky attitude. It's as though he feels he has the right to act this way. He looks at Bryce while walking to the stairs. Trent tries to captures his attention, but he never gets it. Instead Bryce focuses on Omani and that sashay walk. Trent becomes frustrated seeing that Bryce isn't fazed by anything.

"Better not wash your arms. The paint might run," he says.

"*Now*!" Omani says.

Bryce didn't seem to be bothered by the remarks at all. He just slicks his hair back and sits at the edge of a cement block. He places the electric guitar on his lap and begins to play softly. Gabe notices and smiles to himself. Amber sits down, wondering what's going to happen next. She places her head in her hands. Omani and Trent go to the kitchen area.

"What is the matter with you?" Omani asks.

"What are you talking about?" Trent asks with a greasy smile.

"The hair comment and don't wash your arm. What's with that?" she asks.

"Nothing. I just don't think he's a good fit," Trent comments.

"You heard him. How can he not be a good fit? Hell, he even added to the song, which is more than I can say about you. Lately all you want to do is complain. You know you use to be so fun and always cracking jokes. What happened? You're not doing the drugs again, are you?" Omani says.

"*No!* Well, maybe if you invited me to the auditions," he proceeds to say.

"Oh, so that's what this is about. You didn't make the selection. What, I didn't pick one of your friends?" Omani asks.

"Omani, if you want us to be a band I think we should all be part of the decision process," Trent says.

"Okay. See, that's all you had to say instead of picking on Bryce. So cut the attitude. In the future, you and Gabe will be included in all decisions. Okay? You happy? Now can we please play some music?" she says. Trent hangs his head, agreeing but still hesitant.

"What is it?" she asks.

"Brandy broke up with me," he replies.

Omani rolls her eyes and shifts her head from side to side.

"You didn't listen to me, did you? I told you to back off. You can't go around shoving your ideas of what kind of woman she is supposed to be for you. That is conditional. Trent, you need to learn that you can't change people. I'm sorry it happened. But you've got to remember that a relationship is a two-way street. Come on; we can talk later," she says.

They head back downstairs. Amber notices that Trent and Omani have smiles on their faces. She gives a reassuring nod to everyone and gathers everyone back to practice. They all place their hands in a circle and raise them high while screaming in unison. They break and go to their instruments, feeling ready to play. Omani taps her foot with a hand in the air, and on the count of three they all begin to play together. The sound is better than ever. There aren't any more emotional breakouts between the members that night. After a couple of hours, the band wraps it up for the night. Everyone is yawning and stretching.

"Well, I guess we can call it a night. But let's get together again tomorrow night. We don't have much time to get this right. And we actually have a second chance for a first impression. That doesn't happen very often, so let's make it good," Omani says, yawning herself. They all come together again, placing their hands in the circle and then breaking for the night. Everyone heads out to their cars. Gabe thanks his friend for letting them use the basement. Then he heads toward Trent's car.

"Hey, want to go over some last-minute music stuff at my place?" Gabe asks Amber and Omani.

Omani agrees but suddenly has a strange feeling come over her.

"Umm, that would be great, but I think I need some sleep. Thanks anyway. We'll definitely practice tomorrow," Omani says, looking toward the sky.

Amber notices Omani acting differently and wonders what is happening. Bryce goes to his oldie but goodie car.

"See you tomorrow," Bryce says, looking at Omani and hoping for some type of conversation to start.

All she does is give a soft okay response. He keeps looking for a conversation breaker but doesn't receive it. He sighs lightly and closes the car door and then drives off.

"I'll call you," Trent says, getting into his car and looking at Omani.

"Yeah, okay. Have a good night, and just think about the things we talked about, okay?" she says, not looking at him but more at the sky. He just shakes his head, not understanding what is going on, and gets in his car. Trent just takes it as tiredness and drives off.

"Is everything all right?" Amber asks.

"Do you feel that?' Omani asks, still looking to the skies.

"No. What is it?" Amber asks.

"I don't know. It's like a strange heaviness. Maybe I'm just tired. Let's go. Here; you drive," Omani says, opening the car door.

They get in, and Amber starts driving. They have gone a couple of miles when suddenly Omani looks back. It's like the heaviness has suddenly become very intense to the point where she can't breathe. Yet at the same time she is drawn to it such that it's almost overpowering. She can feel tingling sensations up and down her arms that get stronger by the second.

"Stop the car!" Omani says.

"What?" Amber says.

"Stop the car!!" Omani says again.

Amber looks at her sister, bewildered by her behavior. Omani opens the car door, not taking her eyes of something. Her sister looks around, trying to figure out what's happening. Omani gets out of the car, leaving the door open, and walks straight in one direction. It's like something is pulling her. Amber quickly gets out and goes to the trunk. Opening it, she grabs a small duffel bag and quickly catches up to Omani.

"What's the matter?" Amber asks.

"Don't you feel that?" Omani asks.

"Feel what?" she asks.

"There's something in there. I don't know what it is, but whatever it is has strength," Omani says.

In front of the sisters is an old house. There are no lights on, and broken windows stand open. It appears to be abandoned. The front door is partially open, hanging on a hinge swaying lightly in the wind. Omani approaches the door and enters. Amber looks at the spooky place and gasps a little before entering. Suddenly Amber feels what her sister meant.

"That is strong," Amber says.

"Yeah," Omani says. "Do you have a flashlight?"

Amber places the bag down on the floor and unzips it. Then she blindly feels around inside. Then, frightened, she pull out a flashlight and turns it on. She shines it around the room. The walls are bare. There's an old fireplace with some furnishings on it, and pieces of furniture are scattered about; cobwebs are everywhere. There is some food left on a table as though someone left in a hurry. They go into the dining room and see on the floor a large pentagram.

"Somebody left without closing the portal. There is something still here. Do you feel it?" Omani asks.

"Yeah. It's pretty eerie," Amber says.

"Come on. Let's go home and get the stuff," Omani says.

"No worries. It's right here," Amber says, holding up the bag.

"You brought the bag? What if someone had seen it?" Omani says.

"Don't freak out. It was in the trunk," Amber says.

"Whatever, let's just get this over with. This place is giving me the creeps," Omani comments.

They quickly set up a few white candles, placing them strategically around the room. Then Amber pulls out the special canister and the dowsing rods. As soon as she takes out the rods, they start swinging hard.

"Whoa!!" Amber says, grabbing them so they'll stop moving.

Omani lights the candles and then stands by her sister. Amber holds out the rods to guide them. They start to work, and the rods point steadily in one direction.

"That's got to be the portal area," Omani says.

Amber gently opens up the canister to spread the special dust. Suddenly Omani is picked up off the ground and thrown across the room. She hits the wall pretty hard, making a loud thud. Amber's body jolts from the shocking sound, and she quickly turns around.

"Omani!! Are you okay?" she asks.

"Just do it *fast!*" Omani says, trying to get up. "Whatever it is, the strength of it is becoming more powerful."

Every time Omani tries to get up the entity tries to hold her down, and she begins to choke. Amber throws the dust and the portal appears, but it's a different color. It's not white. Instead it's black, outlined with various colors.

"Come on, Omani. It takes both of us," Amber says, holding the dowsing rods.

Omani tries to get up and fights hard. The spirit throws her down, slamming her head hard against the floor. Amber tries to get over to her but finds herself unable to move. Something is holding her in place. Amber tries to get loose but can't. She starts to scream as it wraps tighter around her ankle.

"I will not let you do this to me! You have no power over me, for I love thee," Omani says.

Suddenly the entity lets go of Omani, and she starts coughing. She quickly gets up and dashes over to Amber. While running, Omani hits an invisible wall and falls backward to the floor. The strange red eyes suddenly appear.

"There, do you see the eyes?" Omani says, pointing.

Amber looks up.

"*No!* Come on; you've got to help. Something is trying to push me into the portal," Amber says.

Omani looks at Amber's feet and sees them sliding toward the portal. Omani looks at the dowsing rods and then at the portal, focusing. The rods become erect like last time, and the winds come again. The two entities that are bothering the ladies are being attracted to the portal. They quickly go in, and the portal closes. Amber falls to the floor next to her sister.

"How did that happen? You weren't holding the rods," Amber says.

"I'm not sure how it worked. But I thought about grabbing the rods and it happened," Omani says.

"Our powers. They must be growing," Amber says.

"Yeah, but what are they? We've got to find this third person. I have to be honest: this puzzle Grandma left us scares me a little. Those things were strong. I felt like they knew who we were. Besides that, something tells me that we haven't seen nothing yet," Omani says, getting up and dusting herself off. "Come on. Let's get back to the house. We've got a lot of research to do and still need to prepare for our performance. Why did all this have to happen now at the same time? Welcome to my life." Omani says, flustered.

Later on the same night, Amber is working on some new lyrics for a song. On the other side of the room is the research the ladies had been working on for at least a couple of hours. There are notes scattered about as well as papers sorted in a specific way. They're taking a break, and Amber is tapping her foot on the ground trying to get a rhythm with the words. But then she stops and looks at the spiritual stuff they have been working on. It's hard to focus on the music with this new and strange discovery. Amber sighs and starts working on the music again. At times, she stops and crosses out words and adds different ones, trying to get the right mix. She is still frustrated, thinking about the other guardian stuff. After about fifteen minutes, she puts the piece of music down, frustrated to the max, and closes her eyes to try to get focused. It's so hard with all this guardian stuff on her mind. Then Omani comes downstairs slightly dressed up. She quickly walks past the living area toward the door. Amber opens her eyes and catches a glimpse of her sister.

"Hey, hottie, where you going?" Amber asks.

Omani backtracks without turning around and smiles at her sister. She is wearing a black sexy top and shapely pants.

"Well, after everything today I think I need a drink. You know, to clear my head," Omani says.

"Me too. I'll come with you," Amber says.

"No. Actually, I want to be to myself. I want to think things over. There just seems to be so much happening at once. Plus I feel as though there's a piece of the puzzle missing that Grandma didn't tell us. But before I can think about all that I need to do something to relax or I'm afraid I'll explode. Anyway, when I get back we can talk more, okay?" Omani says.

"Okay, then I'm just going to work on this song," Amber says.

"Great. See you later," Omani says.

About a half hour later, Omani is sitting at a bar listening to some mellow music. The place is almost like taking a step back in time. It looks like an old hamburger joint but with some modern ideas. There are pictures of artists of fifties and sixties time era on the wall. The stools up by the bar have a fifties style to them. There is band setting up on stage. Omani sips her drink and plays with the paper that wrapped the straw. She looks aimlessly about while in deep thought. The crowd isn't too heavy, so the noise level is low. There are some empty stools at the bar beside her. A couple of guys sitting nearby seem to notice her, but Omani is too focused on other things. She sits there just going over a wrap-up of the day in her head. There is just so much to think about; where does she even start? How does one develop logic about something they don't understand?? While in deep thought, she can hear some flirting in the background and giggles silently. It helps break the tension. Omani looks in front of herself, watching the bartender make some fancy drinks. In the meantime, the bar door opens and four people enter at once. One guy heads to the bar, whipping out some cash to pay for a drink immediately. He looks over and sees Omani. As he gets closer to where she is seated he requests a drink. He slicks his hair back and takes a deep breath.

"Hey there," a voice says.

Omani almost chokes on the drink while putting the glass down. She starts to cough uncontrollably for a second. Then she turns around and just stares at the person in front of her. He takes her breath away. For a brief second it's as though the world has stood still.

"Didn't mean to startle you," Bryce says, breaking the silence. "So much for going home, huh?"

"Well, I ... I decided I could use a drink," she says, picking up her glass again.

"Me too. Mind if I join you?" Bryce says.

"Sure. But I don't plan on being here long. I do need to get back home," Omani says, starting to stand up as though about to leave in a rush. Bryce notices and sits down, trying to figure out a way to make her feel comfortable. He slicks his hair back again, trying to be cool, calm, and collected. Then cleverly he lifts his arms, gesturing that he is smelling his pits.

"I did take a shower, you know. No need to get all jumpy. I just want to have a drink like you. Come on; it's on me," he comments with a suave attitude, turning toward the bar.

"Did I come across like that? Sorry. It's just all the pressure of everything," she replies.

"I can understand. You have a band member who leaves just when you need them the most. Then you've got to get me up to speed to get this deal. By the way, how do you think it went tonight?" he asks.

"Great! Are you kidding! It's like you've been playing with us for years. I think you're a definite bonus," she says, sighing as though holding something back.

"So uh ... did that go along with Trent's seal of approval too? I must say he's a little uptight. Is he just not getting any or what?" Bryce asks.

Omani starts laughing. He watches her smile and reaction with great joy.

"Trent is an interesting guy. He means well but can be controlling. We all worked so hard for this. We're just afraid that it could go all away in a split second," Omani replies

Just then the band begins to play. It's not too loud, but the sound is quite remarkable and quickly draws a crowd. Bryce pulls his chair closer to her so they can talk better.

"You know, you need to think about a new hairstyle," he says.

Omani begins to touch her hair and frown at Bryce all at the same time. Then she looks in the mirror at the bar.

"Excuse me? I've had this style for years," she responds, offended by the comment.

Bryce sits up in his chair and coughs. He knows that he is in the hot seat.

"Exactly. You see, I was in a rock 'n' roll band before you. And part of what's important in being discovered is in the personality. Your hair is long and pretty, but it lacks character. You've got spunk and attitude. You need to show it," he says, drinking a shot.

Omani sits there not knowing what to think of the comment. It's hard to even think of a good comeback because she's not sure if it was a compliment or an insult. This guy is quite suave.

"So you think I'm boring," she replies.

"No, not boring. Not expressive. You're an artist. Not only do people want to hear your art; they want to see it. You know, through clothes, makeup, hair, etc. Look at me. I like to express myself with tattoos, hats, and various unique clothing. Take risks is all I'm saying. Being afraid will only hold you back from your true destiny," he says, doing another shot.

She just stares at him. He's a lot deeper than she expected. It's as though he sees right to her soul and doesn't even realize it. It's almost overwhelming. He is just amazing, but at the same time there is an air of mystery. When she looks into his eyes there is a feeling of loneliness and pain; something that is hidden but visible. It's obvious that he doesn't want it to be a point of discussion. The two look at each other like their souls have just met. She doesn't know how to even respond to this strange feeling coming over her. It's beautiful yet frightening.

"Well, thank you for your opinion. But I think I'd better get going," Omani says.

She stands up and begins to fall to the floor. Bryce quickly reacts by putting the drink in his hand on the table and kneeling down to catch her. She lands lightly on the floor and starts to laugh.

"How much have you had to drink?" he asks.

"Just three drinks. Look, I just tripped on my purse," she says.

There on the side of the stool is the purse with its string wrapped around her ankle tightly and also around the chair. He detangles the purse and hands it to her. Omani gets up, limping a little, with a strong indentation in her skin.

"Here. I'll walk you to your car," he states.

"*No!* I mean, I'll be all right. I can deal with it," she says.

"I insist. Please," he says.

She gives him a look of disapproval but allows him to help. His mystical eyes are so inviting. He takes her arm and walks besides her, taking her purse back to carry. When they get to her car she tries to put a little pressure on her ankle and begins to fall again. He catches her, and this time they are face to face. Their lips are millimeters from touching. She looks into his eyes and then at his lips. Bryce looks into her eyes endlessly. Then Omani grabs the side of the car to pull herself up and looks at him again. There are no words spoken; their hearts are racing silently.

"Thank you," she says, trying to stay professional.

"Welcome," he says, handing her the purse. "Guess I'll see you tomorrow."

He begins to turn away slowly as though thinking or plotting something to say or do, but there is just silence. She keeps hoping that he will turn around, but he slowly keeps walking away in the hopes that she will do something. Many thoughts enter her head. She keeps thinking what is it about this guy? No one has ever had this much affect on her, ever. The way he makes her feel really affects her. It's more than just the way they look at each other. Somehow he makes her soul sing, but she doesn't know why or how. She wants to do something to discover why but is scared. What if he rejects her? The thoughts get stronger in her mind to the point of making her want to scream. But in just this second, something in Omani snaps. She can't take it anymore and suddenly grabs Bryce by the shoulders, making him turn around. She braces herself against the car, just looking at him with intense emotion. He wonders what's wrong and so looks at her foot. Omani grabs the belt loop on his jeans and pulls him close. The feeling between the two is so magnetic that their lips meet and they begin kissing. After a second they stop and look at each other. Then Bryce gets closer. He wraps his arms around her and begins to kiss her again but more intensely. They begin running their fingers through each other's hair. Then Omani pushes him back.

"I'm sorry. I shouldn't ..." she says.

"I'm not," he says, placing his finger on her lips to quiet her and then kissing her again.

He begins to feel up her body. She pulls him closer, and they hug.

"My place isn't too far from here," he says.

"But my sister," she says.

"I think she can take of herself. Remember—risks. Let me show you what taking a risk with me can mean. I guarantee that you won't be disappointed," he whispers, kissing her again.

The next thing they know they are on his bed, and Bryce is on top of Omani. Their lips are in a soft caress while their bodies are in harmony. Then he slowly sits up, taking off his shirt. She is gently touching his bare chest and then pulls him close. They begin to kiss passionately again. They roll over with Omani landing on top. They are feeling each other and giggling softly. She begins to kiss his chest, going toward his waist line. He plays with her hair, sighing in enjoyment. Bryce's eyes almost roll back in his head from the bliss of it all. When his eyes focus again, he looks off to the side of the bed. Suddenly he jerks away from the side of the bed to the center. Omani stops what she is doing, startled by the commotion.

"What the hell is that?!!!" he shouts.

Omani, stunned by the statement, looks out away from the bed. There in the dark are the two red eyes again. There is no face, just eyes staring at Omani and Bryce.

"You can see it!!!!!!" Omani says.

Bryce pushes Omani off him and puts her behind him as a protective instinct. He tries to hit it with his arm, but it doesn't work; the eyes don't even flinch.

"Get away from me," he says, backing up further in the bed.

"Oh my God. You can see it!!!" Omani says, all excited.

"What do you mean I can see it? *What the hell is it!*" he screams.

"I don't know. But no one else can see it but you and me," she comments, almost in tears.

The eyes suddenly disappear, and Bryce jumps up and runs to the door, flicking on the lights.

"Okay, do you want to explain this to me? Why aren't you freaked out? Didn't you see those eyes? They were red and vicious looking," Bryce says, trembling.

"I know. I know. Bryce, it's okay," she says, trying to be calming. "I've seen them before. They have never hurt me. I'm not sure what it means. I'm still trying to figure it out myself."

Bryce is completely shirtless. He runs his hands through that fantastic hair as a calming mechanism. There are other tattoos on his body that are usually covered by his shirt. One of them catches Omani's eyes. It's a symbol she remembers on one of Grandma's drawings.

"That tattoo. Where did you get it?" Omani asks, approaching him.

"Huh?" Bryce says, looking all of his tattoos over.

Omani comes up to him and points to it.

"Oh, this one. I've had it for years. It's actually part of a birthmark; I added a tattoo to disguise it a little," he says.

"Bryce, I think you'd better come with me," Omani says, startled.

He looks at her, still focused on the last situation.

"What do you mean?" he says, trying to calm himself down.

"That tattoo isn't a birthmark. I've got something I need to show you. It something you've got to see to believe. Come on; there's no time to waste," Omani says, handing him his shirt and bolting for the door. Bryce is stunned by all of this and puts on his shirt while running out the door.

CHAPTER 6

BACK AT THE HOUSE, Amber is sleeping on the couch. Jasper is at the front door meowing loudly. She doesn't hear the cat; instead she rolls over to her other side and sighs. The lights are on, and sheet music is lying on the floor beside the couch with several comments written on it. The guitar is lying on the floor beside the couch on top of its case. The place is very silent. Suddenly the door swings wide open. Jasper runs out before Omani even notices him as she walks in.

"Amber!! Amber!!" Omani says. "Where are you?"

Amber instantly sits up on the couch with her eyes half open. She looks around, just trying to wake up. Omani runs into the living room, and when she sees her sister she starts babbling about something.

"Whoa. Hold on. I just woke up. Give me a minute," Amber says.

She closes her eyes and stretches. Then Amber opens them up and sees a man standing there.

"Bryce! Omani, what are you doing?" Amber asks.

"Come on," Omani says, trying to gesture to her sister to come upstairs.

"What are you talking about?" she replies.

"It's important. I think I figured out something," Omani says, running to the stairs, holding and pulling Bryce's hand.

"Can't it wait till practice?" Amber says, yawning while still sitting on the couch, obviously very upset.

"*No*. And it's not about music. It's about … you know," Omani says, going up the stairs.

Amber's anger quickly dissipates as she jumps up and wastes no time dashing for the stairs.

"Okay, but why is Bryce here?" she asks, not seeing her sister in sight.

Amber gets to the upstairs room and sees Omani rummaging through papers as though looking for something.

"What's going on?' Amber asks, wide awake now.

"*Here!!* Look at this," Omani says, handing the sheet to Amber.

Her sister looks at it, wondering what the big commotion is about. She looks at the picture a couple of times and then at Omani. Amber is beginning to wonder how much her sister drank tonight.

"Okay. You woke me up for this?" Amber says.

Omani goes over to Bryce and lifts up his shirt so that his entire chest is showing. He blushes a little and tries to cover it up.

"No ... for this," Omani says.

Amber sees the tattoo on Bryce's side. Then she looks at the picture. She does this a couple of times.

"Where did you get that tattoo?" she asks.

"He didn't. It's a birthmark. He added this part to it," Omani replies.

Amber moves up close to look at it in detail.

"It's exactly like the picture!" Amber replies.

"Winner winner chicken dinner. And take a look at this," Omani says.

There on a separate sheet are various symbols with meanings written next to them. Amber reads them quietly but aloud. Bryce is intrigued by all of this.

"So I have a tattoo that looks like a picture from that book or whatever. What's the big deal?" Bryce asks.

"You're a Dullet; that's the big deal. It says it right here," Amber replies. "Omani, that means ..."

"Yep," she responds.

"Dullet? What the hell is that? Is it something related to a bullet? 'Cause if that's the case that's how fast it will take me to leave," he states sarcastically.

Both ladies look over the information closely.

"It doesn't define completely what a Dullet is. We're still learning about all of this ourselves. Bryce, has anybody in your family ever talked to you about supernatural or spiritual stuff?" Omani asks.

"No. Oh wait. There was Aunt Bernice. She claimed to have some psychic gift. But everybody thought she was coocoo man. Other than that, no," Bryce replies.

"What gift did she say she had?" Amber asks.

Bryce rummages through his hair with his hands. It's obvious that he is uncomfortable talking about the subject. He sighs a little as though hoping the ladies will change the subject. But they keep looking at him intensely, waiting for a response. He sighs again, knowing that this is no-win situation.

"She thought she could see demons, the future, and how to alter something. I don't know. Nobody really paid attention," Bryce states.

"Where is she?" Omani asks.

"Ahh, she passed away about five years ago," he responds.

"Okay. Well, what if I told you that she wasn't nuts? You saw those red eyes," Omani begins to say when he interrupts.

"That was probably a figment of my imagination. We both drank a little, right? Weird stuff happens to me all the time. Look, I'm not some Dullet or whatever. I think I'd better go," Bryce says, walking toward the room's door.

He shakes his head, wondering what kind of band he just joined. Maybe it's a cult. He's not sure what to think of it all but wastes no time trying to leave. Omani puts the papers down and looks at Amber, horrified. They know this may be a battle. Omani heads to the doorway of the room as Bryce is about go down the stairs, not looking back.

"*Wait!* What if I can prove it to you?" Omani says.

Bryce turns around slightly with great hesitancy.

"Prove what?" Bryce asks, not sure if he really wants an answer. He has one foot almost on the stairs.

"That your Aunt Bernice was right," Omani says, hoping to convince him.

"Look, I appreciate everything. But my aunt was weird. I think you might want to look for a different guitar player. I'm not sure if this band is suited for me," he says with a slight almost frown. This makes Omani nervous. She clenches the doorway woodwork, trying to think of something to say. Amber is in the room listening but standing still. She begins to tap her feet, feeling everything slip away.

"Okay, I'll make a deal with you. Come with Amber and me now. We can show you something that will prove my point. If you're not convinced after that then I'll let you leave the band, no questions asked. However, if I'm right, you'll be open to learning more. Come on. What do you have to lose? Look at it as a dare or challenge," Omani states.

Bryce sighs, looking around unsure of what to make of it all. Omani is still clenching the doorway looking at Bryce with hopeful eyes. Amber feels good about the save but still uncertain about everything else, so she taps Omani's arm and turns to her sister.

"Do you know what you're doing?" Amber asks.

"What choice do I have?" Omani says.

Bryce looks Omani over out of the corner of his eyes until she turns back around. He places his hand to his lips, gently touching them.

"I think I'm up for the challenge. But I would like to add something," he says.

"Name it," Omani replies with great determination.

"If you convince me, I'll listen. But if you don't, no more discussion of this. Plus, you let me take you on a date, no questions asked, and open to suggestions. Deal?" Bryce says.

Omani stands there stunned by the comment and request. Amber is silently smiling and nodding, knowing that this was where it was going. Omani takes a deep breath, knowing he's got her. She gives him a look of intimidation along with frustration.

"Deal. Come on, Amber; get the stuff. Just be careful what you wish for," she says, walking toward Bryce.

"Oh, you mean I get a wish in addition to the date? Now that's what I'm talking about," he says.

"Watch it; things don't come by as easily as you think," she replies.

He watches her go down the stairs with a greasy smile. Amber comes out of the room noticing the look on Bryce's face. She hopes her sister knows what she's doing. This man is suave and knows how to get what he wants. She's wondering if Omani can handle him.

After a few minutes, all three are in the car driving in the dark toward a country area. The city lights become dimmer and dimmer while the darkness increases. Bryce thinks this is nothing and just sits back admiring the view. After they drive for another fifteen minutes, Bryce starts to wonder where they are going. They are in an area where there is nothing. What can possibly be out here? He looks at Omani and gives a quaint grin. He starts feeling a little uneasy, not understanding why, and tries not to show it. The windows are rolled down slightly, so he can hear the sounds of nature, but there is one noise that he doesn't recognize. It startles and scares him. He tries to keep his cool while feeling more uneasy inside. Suddenly the car stops on the side of the road, where there is nothing but blackness.

"Well, we're here," Amber says.

"Where's here?" Bryce asks, looking around and seeing nothing.

"Come on and find out," Omani says, opening the car door.

They get out and look around. The dome light in the car is still on. Amber opens the small duffel bag and gets a couple of flashlights. She hands one to Bryce, and he turns it on and immediately starts to look around. He doesn't notice anything at first but then sees something in the distance.

"Is this a cemetery?" he asks.

"Yes," Omani replies.

"What are you going to do? Dig up the dead or do a séance?" he asks somewhat sarcastically.

"Just come on," Omani says.

They walk deep into the cemetery toward an older section. As they approach it Bryce notices flashes of blue light. It happens every once in a while around the ladies as they continue walking. He doesn't make much of it and just continues to follow. Then a streak of blue light comes at him. He jumps to the side, trying to avoid it, and then watches it as he continues walking. Bryce looks at the ladies, wondering what's going on with them. Suddenly the once silent wind begins to pick up. It has a strange eeriness to it that was missing before.

"It feels different this time," Amber says.

"Yeah, I'm not sure if I like this. Maybe we should go back," Omani replies.

Then off in a distance a dull red light appears. It flickers for a few seconds and then fades. Then it appears again but closer.

"Do you see that?" Omani asks.

"Yeah. What is it?" Bryce asks.

"I don't know, but it ain't good. I can feel it," Omani replies.

"Yeah. Look, there's another one over there and there," Bryce says, pointing.

They hear strange rustling noises plus eerie low-tone almost nonhuman sounds.

"Okay, that's new. What the hell is that?" Amber asks.

"Wow, it sounds awful," Bryce says, stepping back slightly. "Yuk! What is that horrible smell?"

"I think we'd better go. Come on. *Now!*" Omani says.

They all turn around in unison. Right in front of them are those squiggly black things. They snuck up this time.

"Uh, what or who are they?" Bryce asks calmly but terrified.

"Some sort of demons," Omani replies.

"Oh! And I thought it was just my imagination. I think I've seen enough; time to go," he says, starting to walk.

Bryce takes two steps and hits something that knocks him down to the ground. The red flickering lights are closer. Bryce looks over at Omani and Amber.

"Look out," he says.

Omani turns around, and the flickering light thing picks her up and throws her far.

"Oh my God. Omani!" Amber says, getting ready to rescue her.

Suddenly something grabs Amber and forces her to the ground. The thing begins to drag her by the hair. Bryce is lying there motionless, stunned by what he sees.

"*Help!!*" Amber says.

"Amber, I can't get up. It's holding me down," Omani says.

"Okay. Okay. The fun and games are over. Trent, Gabe, I know it's you. Ha ha; very funny. Look, I'm sorry if I bruised anyone's ego earlier. But is this really necessary?" Bryce asks into the darkness.

"Bryce, get the bag!!" Amber screams. "We need the rods."

Bryce gets up smiling and still thinking it's a prank until something comes up behind him. He can feel that something is there. It's giving off a terrible stench, and he has an uneasy feeling. He slowly turns around and sees flickering orange red eyes looking at him above a strange squiggly body. He gulps and is frightened to death. Then it gets to his eye level and looks deep into them.

"You're no Dullet! No one can help you now. You're mine," it says with a strange deep nonhuman voice. It begins to grab hold of his heart and begins to squeeze. Bryce kneels down to the ground in severe discomfort. He makes grunting noises as though gasping for his life. Omani and Amber can hear it.

"Get the bag, Bryce!!" Amber says again.

He looks around while struggling to live and sees the bag almost at arm's length. He reaches out, trying to get it while his breath quickens and the life is literally being sucked right out of him. Bryce can't reach the bag but keeps trying. He nudges himself forward to get closer and sees a squiggly figure heading for the bag. He notices and knows that he's got to get it. He forces himself over more to make one last try. Finally he grabs the bag just as the squiggly thing does, and a tug of war begins. Another flickering light figure comes over toward Bryce. This one looks even more vicious.

"It won't let go," Bryce says with a suffocating voice.

"Tell it you have no power over me and I love thee," Omani says.

"*What!!*" he says.

"Just do it!" Amber says.

He says the line, and suddenly the thing lets go. But there's another one fast approaching. He opens the bag.

"What am I looking for?" he asks.

"A canister and rods. Hurry!!!" Amber says. "*Omani, I'm going into a portal! Help!!!!*"

"*Hurry, Bryce!!*" Omani screams.

Bryce looks around in the bag but doesn't see anything, so he dumps it out on the ground. Looking up he sees that the thing is only a few steps away. He quickly sees the strange canister and dowsing rods and grabs them and starts running.

"Got it. Now what?" he says.

"Open the canister!" Omani says. "Then sprinkle the dust."

"*What?!*" he replies, thinking *how stupid*.

"*Just do it!*" Omani says. "Oh shit!!"

"What?" he asks.

"It's taking me to a portal too. You've got to hurry, Bryce," she says.

His hands are trembling so hard that it's difficult to open the canister, so he stops running for a second. A thing makes a grab for him, but Bryce ducks and it misses. He pulls hard on the canister, and the lid flies off. He reaches his hand inside and grabs some strange glowing dust and throws it into the air. It seems to have a mind of its own and goes in a specific direction. He is wowed by this and just stands there watching it with his mouth hanging open. Then something knocks him to the ground from behind, and he can feel something trying to grab his hair. He pulls it toward himself and begins to roll on the ground. Suddenly he lands on the rods and grabs them. The flickering orange red entities stop in their tracks. Bryce isn't sure what just happened, but he holds onto the rods for dear life. They start to move on their own. He watches them in awe while also freaking out.

"Umm, Omani, the rods are moving on their own! What do I do?" he asks.

"Do you see a portal formed by the dust?" she asks.

Bryce looks around. He doesn't see anything right away. Then he looks behind himself and sees a strange glow a short distance away that wasn't there before.

"*Yeah!*" he says.

"Okay. Get over here quick!" she replies.

"Keep talking so I can find you," he replies.

Omani continues babbling while holding onto a gravestone. Her body is up in the air starting to be sucked into a portal. There are more and more of those strange squiggly things coming around trying to pull on her, and the gravestone begins to lean toward the ground.

"Amber, are you okay?" she asks.

There's no reply. She repeats the statement; there is still no reply.

"Come on, Bryce!!" she screams.

"I'm here," he says, coming from behind her.

"Okay, point the rods toward that glow over there," she says.

Bryce stands up and holds them in that direction. They quickly become erect. Omani stares at the rods and then the portal as the winds begin to pick up like a storm. The strange entities start getting pulled toward the glowing portal. Bryce watches, thoroughly engrossed and terrified at the same time. After a few seconds, everything is gone. Omani is lying on the ground and takes a deep breath. Then she quickly comes to and gets up.

"Amber!! Where are you?" Omani asks, expecting a reply.

There is nothing.

"Oh my God!! Where's Amber?" Omani says, running around in circles.

"*Amber!*" Bryce screams.

They run together looking for her.

"Her shoes!" Omani says.

She looks up and sees the dark portal with different colors in it. The shoes lie beside it.

"She's in there," Omani says, devastated.

"What do we do?" Bryce asks.

"Come on. Grandma's book is in the bag," she says.

The run back to the bag lying on the ground. The book lies open, and Omani frantically flips through the pages trying to find something. Bryce watches her closely, not knowing what to think of it all.

"Here. It says that the only one who can get her out is a Dullet. Bryce, you have to go in," she says.

"*What!!* I'm not going in there!!" he exclaims.

"You have to, Bryce. It's the only way. In another section it says something about needing rope, and to recite this saying, but it's for non-Dullets. I don't know if as a Dullet you need this, but it's better to be safe than sorry. Now the rope is to be tied to a tree. Then I have to say a protection prayer for you before you enter. Come on," she says.

Bryce just stands there, horrified. Omani is halfway there and notices that Bryce is not by her side. She turns around.

"Would you come on!!" Omani says.

"You've got to be kidding!" he replies.

"Do you want her death on your hands? Then come on. I'll help you," she says.

"I'll never make another bet again," he says, walking toward her.

Omani ties the rope to the tree and hands what's left to him to tie to himself. Bryce ties the rope so tight he can barely breathe.

"Okay," he utters.

"You don't have to tie it that tight," she says, reaching toward him.

"No, leave it," he responds.

" May God protect you," she says.

"Okay. What about the protection prayer?" he asks.

"I just did it," she replies.

"That's it!! I could have said that!" he replies.

"Just go get her. There's no time to waste," she says.

"Okay, I guess I know what my life is worth," he says with great uncertainty.

He begins to walk, and suddenly Omani stands in front of him. He starts wondering what she is up to now; hopefully a longer prayer. She reaches up to him and kisses him on the mouth very deeply.

"Come back with her and the date is still on, no questions asked," she says seductively.

His mouth opens, stunned with excitement. She gently reaches down below his belt and smiles. He gives a very satisfied smile. Then he pushes her out of the way and starts walking toward the portal. His legs tremble with every step, but he is reluctant to show it. When he is almost in it, his body begins to fade away. Omani stands there with tears running down her face.

"God, please keep them safe. They're all I have," Omani says.

CHAPTER 7

FIVE MINUTES AFTER OMANI saw Bryce go into the portal there is no sign of anything or anyone. She looks at the rope; it's perfectly still. She's curious about what's on the other side of that portal. Did the demons get a hold of both Bryce and Amber and kill them? Now six minutes have gone by and still nothing. Omani starts pacing while biting her nails. She looks in the duffel bag and picks up the book. She opens it and starts riffling through, trying to figure out what else to do. But there are so many things running through her mind that she can't focus. She becomes frustrated and drops the book back on the ground on top of the bag. She sighs, feeling hopeless and helpless while starting to pace again. After a few seconds, she walks over in front of the portal. Then she looks at her watch. It's been nine minutes. She releases another sigh as the frustration becomes unbearable.

"That's it. I'm going in," she says, frustrated.

She picks up another rope, shorter than the last, and it doesn't seem to be as strong. But she ties it around her waist and the tree anyway. Then she takes a deep breath and walks toward the portal. Just as Omani is about to enter, she feels a tug on her rope. Omani isn't sure what to think, so she slowly looks back at the tree. There the other rope is moving, hitting her rope. She quickly turns back toward the portal and sees a foot. She starts getting nervous and excited. Then another foot appears. Suddenly she sees Bryce dragging Amber with his hands under her arms

"Bryce; Amber!! Are you okay?" Omani screams, running to their side.

Bryce places Amber on the ground.

"I don't think she's breathing!!" Bryce says, kneeling down to listen.

Amber is covered in thick black soot, so much that they can't even see her face. The soot smells and looks funny too. It has steam rising off of it, and it feels ice cold. As the smell becomes more pungent, the grass and flowers nearby begin to wither and die. Bryce and Omani can't help but notice and look at each other in fear. Bryce leans forward again to listen to Amber, realizing the seriousness of the situation. Omani gets down with Bryce to listen; they both hold their breath.

"Anything?" Omani asks.

"I don't know. I can't tell with all that stuff all over her. Wow! This stuff stinks!!" he says.

"Don't breathe it in!!" she replies.

He rips off his shirt and starts wiping Amber's face. Then he puts his ear close to her mouth and nose, holding his breath.

"Anything?" Omani asks, terrified.

Then Amber starts coughing.

"Give me your shirt," he says.

"What?" she asks.

"Look at her. We need to wipe her down or she might choke, or worse yet breathe it in," he says.

Omani quickly takes off her shirt. He wipes Amber down more diligently but also tries to take a few glimpses at Omani's breasts even though she's wearing a bra. Amber starts to cough and then opens her eyes.

"Thank God you're all right!" Omani says.

"What takes you so long? Ooh!! What's that smell?" Amber asks.

The other two start to laugh and hug while tears build up in their eyes.

"We can discuss things after I get you home. I think you need a shower, and fast," Bryce says.

Amber feels her clothes and notices the soot. She is disgusted and wipes her hands on the now dead nearby grass, trying to get it off. But the stuff sticks like glue to the skin. They help her up and quickly head for home.

When they get back to the house Amber dashes for the stairs, trying not to touch anything, including herself. She moans and groans the whole time with high anticipation of getting in the shower. The bathroom door slams shut. Omani is trying to remain calm by combing both hands through her hair. Bryce is admiring her from a distance while drying his hands after washing them vigorously. It's obvious that Omani needs something to calm her nerves. Tonight has been quite traumatic; so much so that she sits down without really caring where and lands on the edge of the sofa. She stares at the floor while her mind wanders. A small smile comes across Bryce's face. He tiptoes to the door, quietly leaving it open. Omani just sits there without moving an inch. Bryce comes back in silently, walking to where she is sitting with an acoustic guitar. In the center of the living room there is a wide-open space with a beautiful, elegant rug. Bryce sits down in the center of the rug with his guitar in hand. Omani notices him out of the corner of her eyes and looks in his direction. He smiles, holding out his hand and inviting her over. With no words spoken she sits down next to him. Bryce gently takes her by the hand and guides her to sit directly in front of him. Omani crosses her legs, getting snug. Then Bryce wraps his legs around hers.

"It's okay. Just relax and listen," he whispers very softly.

Bryce takes the guitar and places it in front of both of them. He takes her hand and places it on top of his. Then he places his chin on her shoulder. Omani can feel each breath gently embrace her neck. Bryce strums the guitar slowly and intricately. A romantic, seductive sound fills the room. Omani closes her eyes, enjoying the soft beautiful sound. It is so mesmerizing that neither of them moves from their positions. Although they are not kissing, it's like their souls are making love. Omani loses herself into Bryce and basically forgets about the traumatic evening. After about fifteen minutes, he gently stops playing and holds onto the guitar, kissing the back of her neck softly. She slowly turns toward him. He places the guitar down beside them and then gently leans her back to lie down on the rug. They start kissing very passionately. He carefully embraces her face, feeling her soft, glowing skin. They gaze into each others' eyes, falling in love. Suddenly they hear the bathroom door open. They sit up, trying to assume a more casual position as they hear Amber coming down the stairs. Bryce gets up and picks up a piece of information about all the supernatural stuff.

"So where do I fit into all of this?" Bryce asks.

Omani gets up and goes to where he is standing. Their hands grasp each others', and they squeeze hard, like a quiet love embrace. Then she looks over what he is viewing.

"It says here that there is a third, unrelated person with a special purpose. This person will have this symbol, which you have, but it doesn't describe the reason for it. Anyway, the three of us together are supposed to do something about some great evil entity that has been or soon will be released. The question is where and when. Bryce, you're the third person. You proved it by going into the portal. Now we have to figure out where we're supposed to take care of this thing and figure out the meaning of that symbol," Omani says.

Bryce looks over the documents, further realizing their relevancy. He's shocked and afraid. As he looks over the stuff more, Amber comes in the room all refreshed. She has on some comfortable clothing and has wet hair. Omani turns around and notices her.

"Hey. Feel better?" Omani asks.

"Yeah. That was weird. I just got off the phone with Kyle telling him everything," Amber replies.

"Good. So I hate to ask, but what was it like; you know, to go into that portal?" Omani asks, curious yet scared of the possible reply.

"I don't know. When I entered I felt like there were a million hands trying to grab me. There was a long tunnel, and they were trying to pull me down. I felt something like razors touching my skin everywhere. It was awful. The tunnel looked endless, but something was holding me and keeping me from going down it. I don't know what, because there was nothing to hold onto at all. I felt dread and despair. All I can say is that it was horrible," Amber replies.

"Well, after tonight, I say we figure out everything before going on any more adventures. This is just too serious. Plus it seems like with each situation we deal with, the stronger and more severe it gets," Omani says.

"I guess if I had just listened ..." Bryce begins to say.

"You didn't know, but now you do. It's okay," Omani says.

"This is fascinating stuff," he says, picking up more items.

He reaches into a box and takes out an old pair of glasses. He holds them up and laughs. He tries to put them on, but they don't fit his face. So Bryce keeps trying to make them work somehow. They look like a pair of glasses to use as a joke. He likes unique things and looks the glasses over, closely admiring the strange craftsmanship and artwork. They have unique engravings on the side with different metals twisted around each other. The engravings are carefully designed and slightly heavy for glasses.

"Grandma's glasses. Remember these, Omani?" Amber says, grabbing them from Bryce.

"Yeah, whenever we would go out with Grandma she insisted on wearing those even though her vision wasn't bad," Omani says.

Bryce chuckles, looking them over from a distance. He decides to keep his comments to himself. Amber looks the glasses over, marveling at them. They bring back some memories, and she holds them up and looks through them. Then Amber puts them on and starts laughing. Omani turns around and sees them on her sister and bursts out laughing too. Bryce also looks and can't hold the laughter anymore.

"Now those are some granny glasses," he says.

Amber looks at the table, the floor, and the sofa, laughing. Then she turns around holding them on. Her laughter comes to a sudden halt. She takes the glasses off and then puts them back on again. She repeats this two more times. Bryce notices Amber behaving strange.

"What's the matter? Are they leaving a dent on your nose or something?" he asks, laughing.

"Omani, come here," Amber says seriously.

"What?" she replies in good spirits, looking over Grandma's things. Amber doesn't respond any further, so Omani puts the stuff down and then turns around to see what's going on with her sister. Omani notices the smile on Amber's face being replaced with concern and fear.

"What is it?" she asks, getting up from the table and walking over to her sister.

"Take a look for yourself," Amber says, handing the glasses to Omani. "Look over there," she says, pointing.

Omani carefully puts the glasses on and looks at Bryce first. Then she looks in the direction that Amber indicates. It looks as though someone is standing there. She takes the glasses off and looks. There is no one there. Then she puts the glasses on again and sees somebody there.

"Bryce, would you go over by the stairs, please," Omani asks seriously.

He shrugs his shoulders, seeing that they are concerned about something. Bryce walks toward the stairs. Omani still has the glasses on. As he approaches the stairs the person standing there moves away. Omani quickly takes the glasses off and looks. Again there is nobody there. She puts the glasses on and sees the person in a different spot watching them.

"Okay. These aren't ordinary glasses," Omani says.

"Why? What are you seeing?" Bryce asks.

"I think these help to see spirits or something. Here Amber; look," Omani says, handing the glasses back.

Amber looks in the spot she previously viewed. The person isn't there anymore, so she keeps the glasses on and sees something moving. She quickly looks in that direction and sees a spirit moving.

"I think you're right," Amber says, filled with excitement.

"What? I want to see," Bryce says, coming over.

"Don't break them," Omani says.

He takes the glasses and looks around and sees the same thing.

"Whoa!! It just moved," he says, stepping back, petrified. "This is some serious stuff! How is this possible? Where did she get these?" he asks, taking the glasses off and looking at them closely.

"I don't know. She's had them as long as I can remember, and that's our whole lives," Amber replies.

"So what are your thoughts on your Aunt Bernice now?" Omani asks.

"This is heavy. You said I was a what?" he asks, sitting down slowly, stumped by all of this news.

"A Dullet," Omani states.

Bryce goes through documents again that are laid out on the table and starts reading them more slowly.

"Hello there," Amber says, waving.

"Don't talk to it. We don't know if it's good or bad. I think we've dealt with enough tonight. Let's research this a little more. You take this stack; I'll take this one. Bryce, you take this one. Then let's compare notes tomorrow after practice. Remember—not a word to Trent or Gabe. I don't think they'll understand. And we can't afford to lose any more band members," Omani states.

The next day in the early evening the band is in the makeshift recording area of Gabe's friend's basement. They are all practicing, but something just isn't right. There are three guitar players, and Bryce is very good. In fact, he's so good he can play for three people in one. As they play the music it seems like the guitars are competing. Trent is trying to continue but is getting frustrated and more uptight with every note. He shrugs his shoulders, moves his head around, and closes those eyes. But it is becoming too much and fast.

"All right, stop!" Trent says, standing up with his hands on his hips.

Omani and Amber turn around and look at Trent, wondering what all the commotion is about. Omani is standing with one hand on her hip and the other on her waist.

"What's wrong, Trent?" she asks.

He shrugs his shoulders, trying to keep his composure through the frustration. Then he drops his arm to his side, shocked that no one else is getting it.

"Duh! The sound is off," he says.

"What do you mean off?" Omani asks. "We're doing fine."

Trent glares at Omani, refusing to back down.

"No, he's right," Bryce says, backing up Trent.

Omani and Amber look at him in shock.

"Mind telling me how?" Omani asks.

"There are too many of us playing the guitar. It is like a battle zone of competition. I feel like it's the loudest one wins versus a harmony. Can we try something different? I know I'm new and everything, but hear me out," Bryce suggests.

Omani stands there with her mouth partially open feeling slightly offended. Amber put her guitar to her side and looks at Trent and Bryce in disgust.

"Depends on what it is," Amber replies.

"You remember that we were talking about risks?" he says to Omani, "I want you to just sing and leave the guitar out for the next song round. Trust me on this."

"You saying I suck, or what?" she asks.

"No. There's too much going on; the song is getting lost. That's what Trent is trying to say," Bryce explains.

"That's exactly it," Trent responds, feeling understood.

Omani shrugs her shoulders in agreement although very hesitant. The hurt feelings come out when she puts the guitar down and grabs the microphone hard. No words are spoken. She looks at the rest of the band ready to play. They all count to three and begin. At first the hurt attitude comes through in Omani's voice. But then she let it go and gets into the song. When they finish the song everybody looks at each other in amazement.

"What did you think?" Bryce replies.

"You and Trent definitely have an ear for music. I never realized that it was too much to have that many guitars going at the same time," she replies.

"We can rotate," Bryce says.

"Are you kidding!!? You rock with that guitar! Let's play some more tunes and see how it sounds," Omani responds.

Just as they are about to begin the phone rings in Omani's pocket. She takes it out and answers it off to the side. The band members look at each other, knowing something is up. She gets off the phone and joins the group.

"What's up?" Gabe asks.

"That was one of the agents. If we want her to see us we have to play this weekend. She heads out next week for Florida. That only gives us three days," Omani says, sighing.

"We're going to do this! Instead of letting it get to us, let's play to get it right," Bryce replies optimistically.

They continue playing for a couple more hours and then wrap it up. Bryce, Amber, and Gabe head upstairs. Omani and Trent are still downstairs.

"Do you honestly think it's going to happen?" she asks in a very serious tone of voice.

"Look, we're doing all we can. If it's meant to happen it will. But the self-doubt has to stop or it will hinder all of us. You taught me that. Omani, you're the one who brought us together. Now take us to the next level," Trent replies, getting up and beginning to put his drum sticks away.

Omani heads upstairs, realizing that Trent is right. If she gives up, they all do. She has come too far for that. She opens the door to get to the car. There outside the car are Bryce and Amber talking softly, almost in a whisper. The other guys just take off. Omani approaches the other two, yawning from being so tired. Amber looks at her sister in a serious, concerned way.

"Hey, you ready to call it a night?" Omani says to Bryce and Amber.

"I think we need to meet like we discussed last night," Amber says in a rather adamant tone of voice.

"Look, we practiced longer than we anticipated; can't we do it tomorrow?" Omani says, yawning again.

"Omani, I think Bryce discovered something we both missed, and it's important. He was just telling me a little bit. I think we need to listen," Amber says.

Bryce has in his hands the notes he has jotted down. It looks like there are several pages of them. There at the top of one page of notes it says in big letters; powers. Omani's jaw drops. She realizes that he did find something. The yawn that is starting to come on instantly stops, and she tells them to get into the car and head for the house. The items in those notes are about to change their lives forever.

CHAPTER 8

Tʜᴇʏ ᴀʀʀɪᴠᴇ ʙᴀᴄᴋ ᴀᴛ the house and can't get in the door fast enough. Even Jasper runs in the door between their feet meowing. The cat looks at the ladies, purring loudly and trying to guide them toward the kitchen for food. Omani picks up the kitty to give it some love. Then she takes the cat to the kitchen to open a can of wet food. Bryce goes to the table and immediately starts laying out the papers so that the ladies can look them over. Amber starts to read without even sitting down. It is that fascinating. Omani comes out of the kitchen to the table.

"So what do we have?" she asks.

"I think you'd better sit down," Bryce says, holding some papers in his hands.

Amber looks at her sister, nodding and pulling out a chair for herself. Omani slowly approaches the table, unsure of what's going to be revealed. She's not even sure if she wants to know. It sounds so intense; maybe it's not such a good thing. She pulls out a chair, looking at Bryce suspiciously. He just looks back with a serious intent and an almost childlike anxiety to spill the beans. He fidgets with the paper, waiting for the ladies.

"Okay, I may regret saying this, but out with it," she states.

"Okay. After last night with the glasses' incident I looked over some of the documents you had out. Then of course I have these that we separated out. I compared them to the ones I looked over for review. There's a code, and it is done very carefully so it doesn't fall into the wrong hands. But I think I cracked it. Here, look at these documents," Bryce says, scattering them out to be clearly seen.

Both ladies get close up to the table to look them over.

"Do you see anything yet?" he asks.

The ladies continually stare at the documents, hoping it will just dawn on them. But there is nothing. They both sit back and look at Bryce, shaking their heads no in great curiosity. Omani's feet twitch from excitement and fear.

He puts another document down in between the current ones on the table.

"There. Now do you see anything?" he asks excitedly, almost ready to explode from the thrill of it all.

The ladies look again and still shake their heads no. This time they look at Bryce, bewildered and wondering what the heck he is seeing. He notices the look and can't help but chuckle.

"Okay, I can see that the anticipation and suspense is killing you. Do you see these numbers here? They're real small and almost easily missed. Almost ..." he says.

The ladies lean in again.

"Yeah. I see them," Amber replies with Omani quickly following.

Bryce takes out another document and shows it to the ladies.

"Now what do you see on here?" he asks.

They both look diligently.

"Nothing," they both respond.

Bryce nods, grabbing the piece of paper, and gets up. He goes over to the lamp in the corner and starts to unscrew the light bulb. The ladies look at each other, wondering why the sudden urge to unscrew a light bulb.

"What are you doing?" Omani asks.

"Just wait," he says, taking out a light bulb he brought and screwing it into the lamp. The ladies just watch in suspense, looking over the one piece of paper. He turns on the lamp and then goes to other parts of the house and turns off the other lights. Omani does not look pleased. Bryce comes back to the table and whips out another piece of paper.

"Okay, now look," he says with a big grin.

Their jaws drop. They can't believe their eyes. There on the sheet is some writing that could not be seen in basic light.

"I have a black light at home that I use sometimes when I play. And that's how I stumbled upon this revelation. Now on this page you see the numbers again. They're paired with symbols and various strange sayings. This is the page you both dismissed as unimportant gibberish.

But come to find out it pulls it all together," Bryce explains, so excited that it is exhilarating.

Omani looks at him in awe. Amber is dumbfounded and bewildered.

"Go on," Omani says, wanting to know more.

"Okay. I went to a special book store today and picked up this book. It has the same items in it. This book is rare and hard to find. In fact, the owner forgot he even had it. I showed him this one page, and it triggered his memory. Nobody has ever wanted the book, so he just gave it to me. So before practice today I flipped through it. Lo and behold; I got it!!" Bryce says, feeling special and well educated with his discovery.

"*What!!!*" the ladies say, on the edge of their seats with anticipation.

"This is where it gets interesting. Let me go over the book first, then the rest of this stuff. Trust me, it all ties in. Okay, the book states there are different hierarchies amongst angels and demons. Amongst the hierarchies are three spheres; and as the number increases so does the hierarchy. Each sphere has rules to abide by. These rules are created by the dominions. Their entire role is very complicated. Anyway, aside from all of this it goes on and states there are people who walk the earth that are given special gifts by God. These people are like angels but in human form. And those gifts will be called upon when it is time by God. Now, the dominions left them rules to abide by too; which must be found and protected. The book goes on stating there are two people that will be given special rare gifts that are to be highly regarded. The first gift is called Vuex. It is a gift that the archangels oversee. The other gift is a unique set of abilities given to a person to protect the individual with the power of Vuex. This person is called a Dullet. Interesting huh? Anyway, this information has been kept from mankind because of its overall extreme power. The power is so strong that if it falls into the wrong hands it can leave the spirit world in anarchy. Now, here's the scary part, in the hierarchy of demons, only the highest level has the capability of taking the power of Vuex. The highest level is very powerful and dangerous. They can't get this power or it will change the world, as we know it, forever. Now, when the power of Vuex is activated the heavens will collide, the earth will rumble, and the seas will tide. Amazing isn't it?" he asks with excitement.

"Wow!! Go on!," Amber says.

"So, what does this have to do with the stuff grandma left?" Omani asks scared to know the answer.

"That's what I'm getting to next. Okay this area here, where you think it's just a saying? it's not. When I put it all together I found that this is what it means. There are three of us. And each of us has certain powers. These numbers, pictures, documents, and this book tell us what they are. You, Amber, have the power to detect presences near and far. However, you don't have the special gift of sight to see all of them. You can sense when one of us is in trouble; plus you have the ability to initiate telecommunication, which means speaking with your mind and not your mouth. The last power is that you have the special voice. You can chant things that only spirits can understand. That's because your vocal chords are a bit different from the average person's. With this gift you can command specific spirits and control them in difficult times when needing help. When you're scared or extremely worried your vocal chords make a special sound that only specific spirits can hear. Omani, your powers are that you can combine the past, present, and future to guide us as guardians in decision making. Those glasses aren't just for seeing spirits. You need to light an unscented candle and focus on it with the glasses. If you chant the specific words on this sheet the answer to a specific problem will come to you. The smoke from the candle forms an image that only you can see. Or you can use the power of the sun during the day while using or wearing the glasses. Your second power is that you have the ability to manipulate things with your mind when dealing with the supernatural. It's not telekinesis but rather more about using the energy from the environment to make things happen when there are negative entities around. Your third power is that you have the ability to receive messages and communicate with the dead in your sleep and while awake. It's a special and different form of telecommunication. Is this cool or what?" Bryce says, excited and waiting for a response.

The ladies sit there with their mouths open, not knowing what to think. They look at each other, amazed by it all.

"That explains it; how I was able to help with the rods in that house without being able to hold onto them. Wow, Bryce!" Omani says.

"Yeah. It's starting to make sense," Amber replies.

"So, what about you?" Omani asks.

"Well, there's more about you, Omani But all right; this is where it gets real interesting. I have a special ability that keeps any negative entities from entering my body while using this power. My power is that I can create electrical energy from the forces around me to help create portals. The portals I create are used for protection purposes. We can enter them, but the negative entities can't. The second power I have is that I can create force fields that block out negative energy for short periods of time. And my final power is of course that I can enter any portal good or bad and I am protected. You two, however, are not. You can only enter the ones I create. Anyway, what do you think?" Bryce asks.

"You got all of this from that?" Omani asks, bewildered and stunned.

"Yep," he replies.

Bryce throws the book on the table so they can look it over. They both grab for it. Amber flips it open and it immediately goes to a page about powers and sees that the symbols are there. The ladies look at them carefully and then at the documents. They nod their heads and look at Bryce. He has proved himself time and time again. Omani is impressed with him but tries not to show it too much. In fact, she kicks herself a little for not thinking about all of this herself. She looks at the book and documents again, completely mesmerized. After a few minutes she sits back in the chair in deep thought and then looks at Bryce.

"So this is all our powers?" Omani asks.

"Not all of them," he says hesitantly

"What do you mean?" Amber asks, looking at Bryce, concerned.

Bryce stands there not knowing how to tell them the next part. He has another piece of paper in his hands. He opens it and looks at it and then at Omani. She looks at him, trying to figure out his hesitation, and then at Amber. They both shrug their shoulders. Then Omani looks back at Bryce. He sighs running one hand through his hair

"Look, Omani, there's something I need to tell you. This isn't going to be easy, so brace yourself," he says.

Her jaw drops, horrified by the statement. She sits forwards toward Bryce, biting a nail. This highly nervous side of Omani rarely comes out, but this supernatural stuff has everyone on edge. Amber's eyes enlarge like softballs, wondering what is so big that it requires such a statement. She places a hand on Omani's shoulder as a form of comfort.

"What is it, Bryce?" Omani asks with her voice trembling.

"According to this book, you have a very special power. You have the power to see. Not just for solving specific problems like we talked about, but also to see the energies of positive spirits and demonic entities along with the rays of light that surround them. They are special colors the naked eye can't see, but you can. These colors possess a special power that only you can access. It doesn't explain what these special powers are, but no spirit, good or bad, has access to it. It's called Vuex. Your power is so strong that it is considered highly supernatural. The problem is that the demonic entities know that you have this gift, and they want it. According to this book there is a way they can get it, and if they do, the spirit world will be in anarchy. It will change things forever. They can't have it," Bryce says, looking at her, concerned.

Omani laughs a little as a coping mechanism. She looks at Bryce and Amber and sees that neither of them is laughing. She stops and coughs to gather herself quickly.

"Bryce, you've got to be wrong. I've never been able to speak to dead people in my life, nor have I seen any colors other than what all of us can see," she replies.

Bryce pulls out a chair and puts it next to her and sits down. He takes a deep breath, looking right into her eyes.

"Last night was no accident. Omani, some of your powers were activated, and they know it—those red eyes. You said that you're the only one who can see them. That's true. However, a Dullet can see them too. Those eyes are of a high demonic power. They've been waiting to see when your powers would become active, especially Vuex. What I'm saying is you're in great danger. The great entity you talked about being released has been, and for a while. It wants to take your powers before you know you have them or what to do with them. That's why it took Amber in. It was a trick. Obviously it didn't work. This thing is on the loose. It's going to take all three of us to put it back where it belongs. Last night, because we didn't know everything yet, I think I released something else through that portal. Omani, you can't be without one of us at any time," Bryce states.

Omani immediately jumps up from the chair and starts pacing the room with her hand on her forehead while she looks down to the floor. Amber looks at Bryce, shocked.

"Are you certain?" Amber asks.

Bryce nods his head and picks up the book. He flips through some pages and then comes to a stop and lays the book back down on the table, open. There it describes the person with the special gift. There is a caricature of a woman that looks a lot like Omani. It goes into detail about the gift.

"Bryce, what are we going to do?" Amber asks.

"I'll tell you what we'll do. Nothing. Because this can't be right," Omani exclaims, slapping a hand on her thigh.

"Omani, I know ..." Bryce starts to say.

"No, you don't know. None of this would have happened if we didn't open that damn chest. I say we put everything back and seal it shut. Then we recite some prayer and just forget about it," she says, almost ballistic.

Bryce gets up from the chair and goes to her side. She has silent tears falling and, frustrated, she puts her hands up, not wanting him to come any closer. He pushes her hands aside and takes her into his arms. At first she holds her arms limp by her side. But then she wraps them around Bryce and holds him tightly. He whispers to her that it will be okay and kisses her softly.

"I'm going to protect you. That's why we're together. We can put it back in," Bryce says.

"But how?" Omani asks, scared to death. "Are you sure that I have this power?"

Amber gets up and approaches them with the book open to the same page where Bryce left it.

"He's right, Omani," Amber says, showing the pages to her.

The picture of the woman leaves Omani's face frozen in fear.

"*That's me!!*" Omani exclaims.

Bryce holds onto her tighter while she just stares at the picture endlessly.

"Okay, so we know who and what we are now and about our powers. Now what?" Amber asks.

Bryce breaks away for just a second from Omani, still holding onto her loosely.

"We need to activate all our powers and figure out how to make them strong. Then we need to work as a team. Plus, we need to find those rules left behind by the dominions. Look, if just one of us isn't up to par, it can cost us," Bryce says.

Omani breaks away from Bryce, placing her head in her hands while thinking. She quickly wipes away the tears and then turns around and looks at both of them.

"We need to recite a reading I found in the chest. I know what it means now. Come on," Omani says.

They all head upstairs.

There is a window open just a crack on the main floor. Jasper comes out of the kitchen licking his chops after eating. He sits down in the middle of the floor in the hallway where everything in the living room can be seen and begins to clean himself. A small breeze picks up, and the blinds on the opened window begin to move. Jasper stops licking himself and looks toward the noise. A dark flowing figure wiggles itself into the living room through the window. It has those strange red eyes. Jasper sees it and takes off back to the kitchen. The figure slowly and quietly goes to the stairway. Omani, Amber, and Bryce are in the special room where the chest is located. Omani opens it up and starts rummaging through everything that is in it—some knickknacks, family pictures, and spiritual things. Omani keeps looking but isn't having any luck. Amber comes up beside her and starts to help on the other end of the chest.

"What is it that we're looking for?" Amber asks.

"An old piece of paper with a saying written on it in different colors of ink," Omani replies.

"Okay, yeah. I've seen that a couple of times," Amber says.

They keep looking together.

"Ahh, here it is," Omani says, pulling it out.

Bryce is flipping through the book while Omani unfolds the piece of paper. Amber gets up and stands closer to Bryce.

"What are you doing?" Omani asks.

"Looking for the chapter on codes. Here it is," he says. "You said it has different colors of ink?"

"Yeah? Right here." Omani says almost speechless.

"This is no accident either. It's another hidden code. The words written in orange are the ones to recite in their exact order to obtain the powers. Then we have to recite the words in green in their exact order to ask for the powers to grow in intensity. It says here that we need orange and green candles; one by each window with only a small crack to allow the flow of energy. Then we have to hold hands in the center of a main room in a circle facing each other. The words have to be said in perfect timing. Then we hold hands for five minutes with our eyes closed while receiving the powers. Got it?" he says.

"Well, that explains some of the different color candles Grandma has in the chest," Amber replies.

They all head back to the chest, grabbing the candles. Omani stops for a second and leans over with a few candles in her hands.

"You okay?" Bryce asks.

"Yeah. I'm counting how many windows there are. It has to be every window?" she asks.

"That's what it says," Bryce replies.

"Well, there's one downstairs that I don't think is going to budge. Including that one, we need fifteen candles," she says.

They all count what they have in their hands and only find fourteen. Then Bryce moves a woven blanket out of the way and finds another one and holds it up. They all smile, not knowing that around the corner is the dark figure, watching and waiting by a small gap in the door. The trio turns around and heads for the door as the dark entity quickly scurries off. They all start opening the windows slightly, placing the candle with plates under them. Then Omani and Bryce head downstairs and Omani flicks on a light.

"Here's the window I was talking about," she says.

Omani tries to open it but can't. She tries again, making grunting noises. Bryce taps her on the shoulder to get her to step back. He tries a few times and can't get it either.

"Do you have a screwdriver or something?" he asks.

"Yeah. I think so. Just a minute," she says, going to another area of the basement.

Meanwhile, Bryce keeps trying to get the window to open but gets nowhere. Omani comes up from behind him with a small toolbox.

"My dad gave this to me many years ago," she states.

Bryce sets it down and opens it and finds a screwdriver. He picks it up but then sees a small crowbar.

"Ahh, here we go. Stand back," he says.

"Don't break the window!" Omani says.

"I won't. It looks like someone glued and painted here. That's why it won't open. This should help," he says.

Bryce takes the crowbar over to the glued and painted area to nudge it. After doing it a couple of times, he puts the crowbar down. Then he tries to open the window again.

"Presto," he says.

"Well, you're just a jack-of-all trades, aren't you?" Omani says.

"Yes, and I can't wait to show the other trades. That is, if you think you can handle it," he responds.

Omani chuckles. Bryce leans over and gives her a quick kiss on the lips as Amber comes down the stairs.

"Just make sure you change that black light back, okay Jack?" Omani says, laughing.

"Okay. All candles are done up here," Amber states.

"All done here too," Omani says.

"Well, shall we get started?" Bryce asks.

They all smile at each other and head upstairs. The dark figure is hidden under a couch in the living room watching them as they come to the center of the room. All the candles are lit, and the paper with the saying on it is on a small table placed in the center of the living room. The trio looks at each other with hope, fear, and strength in their eyes. The special ceremony is about to begin.

CHAPTER 9

Aᴌᴌ ᴛʜᴇ ᴄᴀɴᴅᴌᴇs ᴀʀᴇ burning in front of a window, and all the windows are opened slightly to let the energy flow. Bryce grabs the chair with the paper on it and places it in the center where they are standing. He places the paper in such a way that all three can see the writing and gestures for them to take a step closer to the chair. The ladies lean in a little to read the writing on the paper, and Amber starts to shiver.

"Can we hurry up and get this done? I'm getting cold," she says.

"Yeah, but you need to know the words because they have to be said in perfect time. Everybody know what it says?" Bryce asks.

Omani puts her hands on her hips while rocking in place.

"Yep. I say we do a practice round just to make sure everybody's gets the words down," Omani replies.

"You read my mind. Shall we begin?" Bryce replies.

Both ladies nod their heads. Just as they are about to begin, Jasper comes into the room meowing very loudly, almost screeching. Everybody looks at the cat, startled.

"I didn't know that the cat knew how to meow. That's the first time I've heard it. Is it sick?" Bryce asks.

Omani gives him a dissatisfied look. Then she walks over to Jasper and bends down to pick him up. She tries to console him. But Jasper jumps out of her arms, still meowing loudly.

"What's the matter, Jasper?" Omani asks. "I just gave you food."

The cat goes into the living room, walking toward the couch and meowing.

"No, I'm not going to hold you right now," Omani says.

"Can you put the cat in a room with the door closed or something?" Amber asks.

Omani picks up the cat again and takes it to the kitchen. She places a chair in front of the door so the kitty can't come out. After a few seconds the cat stops meowing.

"There," Omani says. "Where were we?"

They get into a circle again and look at each other intensely.

"On the count of three, okay? One, two, two and a half, three," Bryce says.

They all look at the paper and start saying the words written there.

"May the gifts that have been in waiting from God be granted to us; our spirits enlightened and intelligence raised. Allow the energy to flow from outside to within, carrying with it the greatness that is meant to be."

After reciting the words they look at each other, almost scared. No words are spoken as they look around.

"Is everybody all right?" Omani asks.

"I think so," Amber replies.

"Well, that went well. Now we have to say it three times in unison and then hold hands for five minutes with our eyes closed. Ready?" Bryce says.

They all nod. Then sneakily the dark spirit comes out from underneath the sofa. Nobody sees it as it goes up the wall closest to Omani and heads to the ceiling. The dark spirit maneuvers until it is right above Omani. The red eyes look directly at her and no one else.

They are beginning to chant the words when the doorbell rings. They all look at each other, startled.

"Anybody expecting someone?" Amber asks.

"No," Omani replies hesitantly. "What if it's Gabe or Trent? Shit!"

Omani runs to the door to look through the peep hole. The person outside is standing extremely close to the door, so she runs to the nearest window to see who is there. It's still difficult to see.

"Who is it?" Amber asks.

"I don't know. I can't tell," Omani replies.

The doorbell rings again.

"Quick—hide the chair and the paper. Oh, the candles. Don't worry; I can make up something. Okay, be cool, Omani," she says, trying to gather herself. She opens the door slowly, trying to peek. Then she turns to Amber with a big grin.

"Is there something you forgot to tell me?" Omani asks Amber.

"Huh?" Amber replies.

"I think this is for you," Omani replies.

Amber looks at Bryce, shocked and shrugging her shoulders. She approaches Omani, wondering what's going on. Omani stands back and gestures to her sister to open the door. Amber slowly reaches out to the doorknob as the doorbell rings again and opens the door so slowly that it makes a creaking noise. Her apprehension quickly turns to excitement as the door suddenly swings open.

"*Kyle!!!!!!*" Amber says with huge excitement.

"*Amber!!!*" Kyle says, entering the house and putting down his suitcases. He has on a T-shirt that says veterinary medicine and a pair of jeans. His boots look like they are specially made for the line of work he is in, and his hair is cut short.

He immediately grabs Amber and picks her up and twirls her around in a circle, holding onto her waist. Omani has tears from all the excitement. Bryce approaches Omani.

"Who is that?" he whispers softly.

Omani turns to Bryce.

"It's Amber's husband," she says. "He's been in Europe and the coast of Africa. He's a specialized vet for exotic animals. They called him on a special assignment. This can mean either it's done early or they got a big job and gave him a small break," Omani replies.

Kyle and Amber are hugging and kissing very deeply. Omani coughs quietly to let them know they are not alone. Amber breaks away, feeling slightly embarrassed in front of Bryce.

"Honey, this is Bryce, the newest member of the band," she states.

Kyle immediately extends his right hand and shakes Bryce's.

"Nice to meet you. So, is he an add-on or a replacement?" Kyle asks.

"Replacement," Amber replies.

Kyle looks around the room and notices many candles burning in front of the windows.

"Is this a new form of concentration, yoga, or am I just in time for something?" he asks.

"It's a new way of meditation for us to focus on specific things," Omani replies.

"I'll explain it later," Amber replies, "So what brings this big surprise? Is your mission complete?"

He looks at the ground and then takes a deep breath. Then he looks at Amber with almost a somber gaze. Everyone knows that it's not good news.

"The job turned out to be bigger than anticipated. They actually want me there for more time than I designated. So I told them I needed to come home to see my wife before I could continue. Phone calls only go so far. So I'm only here for possibly two nights; hardly time for you to pack your stuff to go back to the house that's over an hour away. Omani, is it okay if I stay here to make it easier on Amber?" he asks.

"Absolutely!! Why don't you go ahead and take your bags upstairs. Amber and I were just about to end a meeting," Omani says.

Kyle picks up his bags and kisses Amber while starting to walk. He heads up the stairs happy as can be, whistling. They all wait silently until they hear him enter the bedroom. As soon as the door closes, Omani wastes no time going up to Amber.

"Amber, he's going to find out. Can he handle it?" Omani asks.

"Yeah. Let me talk to him. But let's quickly do this before he comes back down," she replies.

Bryce quickly grabs the chair and the paper and places it in the center where they were standing prior to Kyle's entrance. They take their places, focusing on the paper. Bryce counts to three again, and they start on time. After the third time the trio closes their eyes and hold hands. Upstairs the bedroom door opens, and Kyle comes out toward the stairs with a wrapped box in his hands. He comes to a sudden stop when he sees the three of them in a circle with their eyes closed, holding hands. He just stares, not knowing what to think. Then the trio opens their eyes. Amber looks right at the top of the stairs and sees Kyle just standing there with a shocked look on his face. She quickly exits the circle and goes to the foot of the stairs.

"What is this? Are you doing witchcraft or something? Because if you are ..." he begins to say.

"No! Omani, Bryce, I'm going to call it a night. Come on Kyle. I need to talk to you," she says, heading up the stairs. She walks with him to the room and closes the door.

"Well, I wonder how that's going to go," Bryce comments.

"I guess we'll find out in the morning. Oh, look at the time. It's almost 12:00 AM. Come on; let's blow out the candles. It's so late. Why don't you stay here?" Omani says.

The paper from the chair drops from Bryce's hands when he hears that comment. He looks over at Omani with an amorous smile, but she isn't paying attention. Instead, she's blowing out candles.

"With an offer like that how can I refuse?" he says under his breath.

Bryce picks up the paper and helps blow out candles. They take all of the plates of candles and place them on the dining table. When they are finished, Omani says, "Okay. Well, good night. Do you need a pillow and blanket for the couch?" she asks.

Bryce's jaw drops, not believing what he is hearing. He thinks about the comment for a second hoping it's a joke. But no comment comes afterward, so he looks around, busily trying to think of something fast.

"I save your sister and you're going to have me sleep on the couch? What about the date?" he asks.

She turns around to look at him, taken aback by the comment.

"So this is the date?" she replies.

"Well, not yet. But who says it has to be a one-night date?" Bryce replies.

Omani begins to open her mouth, but he cuts her off.

"No questions, remember?" he says.

Omani gives him a look, knowing that she has been tricked. On the outside she looks slightly upset. But on the inside, she is turned on. This man knows what he wants, and it is very appealing to her.

"Okay, I'm too tired to argue. Come on. I get the right side of the bed," she says.

He wastes no time following her up the stairs. Omani gets her nightclothes and heads to the bathroom down the hall. Bryce pulls back the covers and immediately begins to remove his clothing. He leaves on his undergarment and lies down on the bed, trying out different seductive poses for when she returns to the room. Omani takes off her shirt, covering her face. While she is doing so, the dark figure enters the bathroom, and a part of it reaches out toward Omani, almost touching her on the back. Omani jerks a little as she is taking off her blouse. Then she places the nightclothes on and puts her dirty clothes in the hamper and heads down the hallway. The dark thing follows her. Upon entering the room, she sees Bryce lying seductively on the bed and giggles a little. He gestures with his finger for her to come to bed. She hits the lights, and a small night light comes on in the corner. Omani climbs into bed; the entity stays close by her. Bryce nudges himself closer to her, smiling while reaching out.

"Are you this way with all your women?" she asks.

"No, only the very special ones," he replies, holding her close.

She cuddles in his arms, enjoying it, and he kisses her on the face. Then she gets a strange feeling and pulls away. Her right arm and leg begin to tingle, so she rubs her arms, looking around the room suspiciously.

"What's wrong?" he asks.

"I'm getting a strange sensation," she replies.

"Good, then my mojo's working," he says.

"No, Bryce, be serious for a second. I think there's something in this room. If I have these so-called powers why can't I see it?" she asks.

"All we did is ask for them," he replies.

"But we also asked for them to get strong. Maybe it didn't work," she says.

"Omani, we haven't done anything to test them yet. We'll do that later. Let's just rest. If something is here, I will protect you. Come on; lie back," he says convincingly.

Omani lies back, but slowly. Bryce holds her tight, trying to get her to relax. While trying to calm her down, he notices the large intricately designed dream catcher above the bed, on the wall, and some pictures on the dresser.

"So who are those people?" he asks.

"My family," she replies.

"Why don't you ever talk about them?" he asks.

"It's personal. I have a different family that I don't think most people would understand," she replies.

"Really? You heard about my Aunt Bernice. Does that qualify as different?" he replies.

She laughs and looks at him with intense admiration in her eyes. He places his hand behind her head and gently pulls her forward, slowly kissing her intensely. She lets her guard down and fully engages in him. Then she lies on top of him. They take a break, looking at each other.

"So tell me what's so different about your family," he asks.

She gets off of him and sits up, taking a deep breath. Then she runs her hands through her hair, looking at the pictures.

"Let's see. I have a mother who doesn't understand me and a father who thinks I should be doing something different with my life. You know; the band thing is such a waste of time and energy. I should be punching a clock—have a real job. Never mind my talents. My mom thinks I should surrender myself to some man and be happy. But it has to be to a man she wants for me; not what I want. So that's always been quite a sensitive subject between us. Grandma, on the other hand, was always on my side. I'm a woman on a mission who knows what she wants. So I had to move out to make my own way. It was painful. But I had to do it. Do we really have to talk about this?" she asks, turning around to look at him.

He lifts his eyebrows at her a couple of times in flirtation. She drops back onto the pillow, laughing.

"No. I think you should surrender to me tonight and enjoy it. I promise to make it worth your while. But tell me this: how did you get a house like this?" he says.

"An older lady lived here. She was placed in assisted living, and the family wanted to sell this house quickly. So I waited until the time was right and made an offer. I got it at a price that's way cheaper than rent. Plus, they left the imported rugs and some artwork behind. So there," she explains.

She laughs, getting back on top of him. They begin to make love, and he gently pushes her hair away from her face.

"Omani, I think you're very special. I never thought I would meet a woman like you," he comments, rolling over and getting on top of her and slowly caressing her.

CHAPTER 10

Early the next morning Amber is sitting on the side of the bed talking with her husband. They're both in their nightclothes. Neither one has combed their hair or done anything to prepare for the day. Instead, Amber is trying to explain all that has happened since Kyle left on his expedition. She is telling him about the cedar chest that Grandma left behind. In her hands she holds some documents explaining things. He is trying to understand, but at the same time he looks at her with disbelief.

In Omani's room, she is curled up next to Bryce, sleeping heavily. He has his arms tightly around her and is sound asleep. But he is a light sleeper, so the slightest movement will wake him. On the outside, Omani looks very peacefully asleep. But on the inside, she is having a strangely intense dream. There's a door in the distance that has a lot of haze in front of it, making it difficult to see. The door looks familiar, yet she has never seen it before. Something is drawing her toward it. She drifts in that direction, hearing a soft mellow voice calling her name. She approaches the door and enters. On the other side is a whole bunch of flowers, like a meadow. The colors are lively, and it looks like spring in full bloom. There is a sense of peace, with the sound of trickling water in the background. Omani's face shows a comfortable happy smile. Off in the distance by the trickling water stands what looks like a person but is blurry. Omani asks if she can help, but there is no reply. Instead, the person keeps calling her name with a now more soft monotone moan. She keeps going toward the voice, leaving the flowers behind, and suddenly enters a dark and scary area. It looks as though it's a dungeon waiting to be filled with people. There are spurts of fire and nasty laughter off in the distance along with tormented screams. Omani starts to back up to go the other way, but a wall blocks her. The voice calls out to her again. Omani's breath quickens as the fear builds. She is torn about what to do. She lifts her arms, feeling around and trying to find the quickest and easiest way out. The feeling of doom and gloom becomes very strong along with horror. Then the voice becomes stronger, pulling her toward it; so Omani follows it further and enters another room. This one is white at first and full of a cloudy haze that slowly fades. Omani realizes that she is standing in her own room. There in front of her stands the shadow with the voice. She asks what it wants. Its voice goes from a soft moan to an actual sound of concern.

"Omani, you must wake up. One of them is in the room. The main one is coming, but you must find it first, or it will take you. Begin to use your powers. It will guide you. Omani, you have the power of Vuex. Only you can access it. Go to Zadku's Point. You must begin, because running is not an option. Wake up. You need to wake up! Now!!" it says.

The shadow person starts to slowly appear to Omani. The voice becomes more familiar. She tries hard to focus. Suddenly a face appears with a look of desperation and fear.

"Grandma!"

"*Wake up, Omani!!! Now!!!*" she says.

Omani suddenly comes out of a deep sleep and begins to move. Bryce feels her and starts to wake up. Omani heeds the warning and opens her eyes quickly. She doesn't even give them time to adjust. She is lying almost on her back against Bryce. As she begins to rise up quickly there in front of her is the dark entity looking directly into her face with no fear. Its eyes lock onto hers, and it makes a fast lunge attack at her. Omani jumps up in bed, and it quickly moves and then again is in her face. It goes from a thick dark cloud to a thin haze and begins to approach her mouth and nose.

"*No!!*" she says, trying to back up in the bed.

Bryce opens his eyes, startled by the sudden comment and movement. He sees the dark thing beginning to enter Omani. He jumps up in bed and grabs her, tilting her back. This thing has a hold of her, paralyzing her.

"*Shit!! Shit!! Omani!! ... Amber!!!!!*" he screams.

Amber jumps when she hears Bryce's call for help.

"Stay here," Amber says to her husband.

She runs down the hallway to Omani's room. She's almost there when it hits her—the sudden feeling of something negative. It overpowers her, and its strength is so intense that it's hard for her to move. She has to use lots of strength to keep moving toward the room. For each step forward, it's like something is pulling her three steps back. Bryce sees the dark entity entering further into Omani. He is frantic but tries to think.

"Okay, what is my power?" he says.

He places his hands out in front of him, thinking. Suddenly a strange image appears. It has a bluish-yellow tint to it. He's not sure what to make of it. He looks at Omani and sees that her eyes are changing to red. He tries to grab the entity but gets nowhere.

"Damn it. I'm a Dullet I've got to be able to do something! This can't be happening!!" he says.

Just then, Amber comes into the room feeling heavy winds blowing her hair all around.

"What's going on?" she screams.

"Command it!" he replies loudly.

Amber looks around, feeling a strange negative presence. She knows that Omani is in trouble. Amber tries to communicate with her sister quietly to figure out what is happening. Omani replies with telecommunication needing help, for it is in her.

"I call upon all positive spirits in this house. You're to come to this room and help Omani!" she says.

A white door appears in the corner of the room. Then they see balls of light enter the bed area next to Omani and begin to grab the negative entity and start pulling. Then another negative presence comes into the room. Amber can feel it as it approaches the bed. Bryce sees it and backs up. But when it hits the bluish-yellow tinted light it bounces off and can go no further. The balls of light take the nasty entity and throw it outside the bluish-yellow tinged light. Then the good spirits take off back into the white door and disappear. The negative entities leave. The bluish-yellow tinged light also disappears. Omani sits up in bed and starts gagging and coughing. Amber rushes to her side.

"Are you okay?" Amber asks frantically.

Outside the doorway stands Kyle with his mouth hung open, scratching his head in disbelief.

"Yeah ... It was Grandma," Omani replies.

"Grandma?" Amber says.

Omani sits up in bed in tears, trying to regain her composure.

"Yeah. She came to me in a dream and told me to wake up. That's when I saw that thing coming at me. But before she told me to wake up, Grandma said that I have the power of Vuex. And to go to Zadku's Point. What does all that mean?" Omani states.

Amber mumbles the word, trying to make sense of it. But nothing comes of it. She shrugs her shoulders. Bryce reaches down beside the bed and picks up the book. He starts flipping pages. Then he comes to a big picture with the word Vuex written on it.

"Yeah, remember? We talked about it last night. Here, there's something on it," Bryce says, reading the pages about it quickly. The sisters look at him, waiting anxiously for an answer. Bryce's eyes enlarge as he reads on. Then he looks at Omani and back at the book.

"Okay, it says here that Vuex is a very special power. Only a few people will ever have this," he recites.

"But what is it? It's very vague. Talking about seeing colors and stuff," Omani asks.

"I'm getting there," Bryce says, reading on.

He flips the page, continuing to read. Amber consoles her sister, touching her hair. Kyle is still standing at the doorway just watching. He's not sure what to make of it all.

"Wow!!" Bryce exclaims with excitement.

This gets Omani all charged up. She sits on the side of the bed with anticipation. Bryce just keeps reading but doesn't say anything. The look on his face indicates that he has found something fascinating.

"*What?*" Omani says, eagerly waiting.

"It's your eyes! But before I get to that, it says that you have a special portal in your brain that is active while you sleep. This portal allows you to communicate with spirits and provides the ability to understand any language. But your eyes! This is deep," he says, bewildered.

Omani is becoming frustrated with him stalling. She stands up and goes over to where he is standing and tries to get a glimpse of the book he's holding. He turns away while reading. She slaps her hands onto her hips, staring at him.

"Are you going to tell me, or are we going to play charades?" she asks.

"I'll take you up on that offer later. But first your power. It says here that Vuex is the ability to see what others cannot. But you have the power to make what is unseen seen. There's a part here that is really evasive in explanation, stating the same thing from last night. But what I'm figuring out is that somehow you can change negative entities into something with this power. It takes a special portal to do that, and you're the only one on this earth who has the power to access it. That's all it says about that part. Over here it states that if the negative entities get this evil power they will inhabit the earth," he explains.

"That's just great. So what's with Zadku's Point?" Omani asks.

Bryce continues reading.

"It says here that no one has ever seen it. But according to legend it is where the sun and time meet. This place is sacred, and if the wrong people enter they will not return. That's it," Bryce says.

"That's it? So if we go there with Omani but we don't have this power, what happens to us?" Amber asks.

"Good question. But I'm not letting her go there alone," Bryce replies.

"Maybe we can access her power without it," Amber responds.

"No. Grandma said it has to be done there. And according to the tone of her voice, time is running out," Omani says.

"Guess we'd better get started," Bryce says.

They all stand up when Kyle walks into the room. Amber hears his footsteps and turns around. She stands beside the bed, not sure what he has heard. Bryce looks at Kyle, feeling his disapproval.

"How long have you been standing there?" Amber asks.

"Long enough. What's going on? Amber, you're scaring me," Kyle says.

"I've been trying to explain it to you. There's nothing to be scared of, because, again, we're not witches. We're guardians. It's a birthright we inherited. We protect the living and the dead. Plus we're to protect a special gift that is never to fall into the wrong hands. The reason this is happening is because something big and bad was released. If we don't put things right, the world will be changed forever. Kyle, we can't turn our backs on this. I need your support," Amber says, pleading with him.

Kyle sighs, knowing that Amber would never lie to him. He looks around the room trying to capture strength and understand it all. Then he sees Amber's very intense eyes looking at him, waiting to hear his thoughts. Omani and Bryce look at each other, enclosed in each other's arms. Kyle feels as though his back is against the wall.

"Of course I support you. But I don't understand this hootie hootie stuff. In fact, it scares me, so I prefer to not know what's going on. I will say this: I don't want my wife placed in a situation where her life is in imminent danger. If I lose her my life is over," Kyle responds.

Tears well up in Amber's eyes. She runs to Kyle and hugs him tightly. He holds onto her and places his face in her hair and rocks her in his arms. Then he sternly grabs her arms and pushes her back so he can see her face.

"I mean it," Kyle states.

"I know," she whispers softly.

"Kyle, she's my sister. I'm not going to let anything happen to her. But you need to have trust in us," Omani replies.

Kyle caresses Amber and looks at Omani. He nods his head. Then he can hear his phone ringing.

"That's my work. That means they probably have a flight waiting for me. Call me. I will be home as soon as I can. I promise," he says.

Amber agrees, silently wiping away her tears. Kyle leaves the room as Omani, Bryce, and Amber join in a circle to do a group hug. Then Amber leaves to be with her husband before his departure.

Later that day the band is in Omani's living room. Trent and Gabe are looking over some music and trying to make some interesting twists to impress the agents. They're both playing their instruments and feeding off each other's creativity. Omani is in the back room where the outfits are going over clothing ideas with Bryce. She points to different outfits that she has worn for various performances. One outfit draws his attention, an eye-catching black-and-white zebra print wrap dress with matching long black boots and a black leather trench coat. He can't stop staring at it, as he doesn't find the other outfits as eye-catching. Omani is talking about a different outfit. She turns around, noticing that Bryce is occupied elsewhere. She goes up to him.

"I like this. It's very creative. Like I said before, you need to be more expressive. Think about the music and what it represents to you. Then think about how you can express it to the people so they can feel it just by looking at you. This outfit says, 'I am woman; hear me roar!' It says, 'I'm conservative yet open-minded and sexy, and my feelings have business.' The others aren't as expressive," Bryce says.

Omani looks at the outfit he's referring to in more depth. She starts to think about the message the outfits are sending. Again, it's like he can see into her soul like no one else can. She looks at him and smiles. He kisses her and then begins to feel her body. He gets real close to her ears with his face in her hair.

"I'd like to hear you roar," he whispers.

She giggles softly.

"Hey, are we going to practice or what?" Trent says, standing at the doorway.

Bryce sighs because his little moment was interrupted. He turns to look at Trent to get him to leave. But Trent doesn't take the hint. He just looks at them, waiting for an answer. Omani places her hand in Bryce's.

"Yeah. Only two days left. I was just going over outfit coordination," Omani replies. Bryce still has his hand in hers and guides Omani to the living room, walking past Trent and giving a daunting stare. Trent just snickers back and walks behind them. They all sit in a circle facing each other.

"Okay, as I understand from Trent, you guys made a change to some music?" Omani asks.

"Yeah, we gave it a little more attitude. You know, like Bryce does with his guitar. Take a listen," Gabe says.

They play a number that is dear to Omani and Amber and put the twist in it. The sound is like ear candy. Bryce nods his approval. It gets everyone nodding to the beat of the song like never before. Then Gabe and Trent do a long four-note finish.

"Expressing yourself. I like it. That's what they want," Bryce says.

This gets Amber and Omani fired up. They both stand up, getting in position to perform.

On the count of three they begin. The mesmerizing sound fills the house with spellbinding intensity. The people walking by on the street can hear it and stop and listen. They gather around the house talking among themselves. When the number is finished the band looks at each other, amazed. The people outside discuss how they like it and continue walking.

"This is really coming together," Amber says.

"I can smell that record deal!" Trent says.

"So, for outfit coordination, what do you think?" Gabe asks.

Omani looks at Bryce and smiles. He nods, gesturing to do it. She takes a deep breath, feeling excited.

"I think we should go outside of the box. You know, wear something people aren't expecting. Something that makes a statement without saying a word. So I say everybody go shopping and see what you can find. Then we will meet and discuss. How's that?" Omani asks.

Everybody nods with excitement. Trent gets out his little notebook and starts writing something down. Gabe looks over his shoulder to see what he's doing.

"Something wrong?" Amber asks, looking at Trent.

He has an intense look on his face as though he's mad, and he doesn't respond. Instead he continues writing something. Gabe looks at the band and shrugs his shoulders because he can't decipher it. Omani takes a deep breath, rolling her eyes and thinking that more drama is to come. After a few more minutes Trent looks up.

"I want this," he says, holding up the paper.

Everybody looks intensely at the paper. It's a picture of a dragon playing the drums and breathing fire.

"On your clothes?" Omani asks.

He shakes his head no and then looks at Bryce.

"I want a tattoo," he replies.

Bryce's face lights up.

"I know just the place," he says.

Amber and Omani laugh a little but keep it under wraps. Gabe looks at the band and shakes his head no for himself.

"Great! Well, time is running out. I say we get started and meet back tonight for a short time. Then tomorrow we do a practice show and then do it. It's going to happen. I know it," Omani replies.

Everybody gets up and starts putting away their instruments. Bryce approaches Omani and explains that he will go with Trent. She nods and goes into the room where the outfits are located. Omani reaches out to touch them, thinking. Then she stands back in the center of the room and gives a confident smile, placing her hand by her heart. She closes her eyes and drifts away, letting her creative imagination take over visualizing the performance.

CHAPTER 11

Later in the afternoon Bryce is driving his car with Trent sitting on the passenger side. They are driving past a body of water with a walkway next to it. There are people everywhere. Some are listening to iPods while walking. Others are skateboarding. The area looks very hip. However, ignoring all of this, Trent is examining Bryce's car closely like a hen-pecking mother. He looks over the books, CDs, and various gadgets closely. He even opens the glove compartment. Bryce is aware and just ignores it, trying to admire the view. Trent looks over at Bryce out of the corner of his eye to see his reaction but gets nothing. It begins to frustrate him. Bryce knows something is on this guy's mind, but he doesn't let it faze him. Instead, he turns on some music and just remains relaxed while driving. Trent readjusts himself in the seat when he begins to hear some classic rock 'n' roll. Bryce fiddles with the CD to get it to the song he wants to hear, and Trent begins to scratch his neck and readjust his shirt, becoming very agitated.

"Do you have to do that?" Trent asks.

"Do what?" Bryce asks.

"Mess with the CD. Why can't you just hear the thing in its entirety?" Trent asks.

"Why, when all I want to hear is my favorite song?" Bryce replies.

"Because it ruins the music experience," Trent says, fidgeting in his seat.

"It what? You're way too anal. How did you become a musician anyway?" he replies.

"Excuse me? Well, how did you get into Omani's pants? You're definitely not her type. Did you pay her or something?" he says, sassing back.

Bryce takes a deep breath, realizing that the conversation is going to get intense, and quickly.

"So that's what this is about? You're jealous of me being with Omani?" he states.

Trent sways his head back and forth in extreme frustration.

"I'm not jealous! Are you kidding?" he replies.

Trent looks out the window, squinting his eyes in anger. His lips begin to quiver, and he starts to rub his upper thigh as a calming mechanism. Bryce just sighs again while continuing to drive and turns down the music. He knows he has to address this sometime, so why not now? He begins brainstorming ideas of what to say to Trent.

"What does she see in you anyway? You have strange hair and a bunch of tattoos, and you're full of it. I thought the last guy was bad. Then you come into our band thinking you know it all. You know, we worked hard to get where we are, and you'll probably just ruin it for everyone. I guess I can thank you in the unemployment line," Trent replies with his eyes twitching.

Bryce has his tongue moving around in his mouth to keep his cool while continuing to drive. But then he snaps as Trent starts kicking one of his musical gadgets.

"You break it, you pay for it!" Bryce says, and Trent instantly stops kicking. "Now let me explain something to *you*, Mr. Anal. I'm an artist first of all. I like to express myself. My hair, my tattoos, all of it is a language that tells people I'm open to things and I have a mind of my own. I don't follow the path everyone else does, and I'm proud of it. Second, as far as Omani goes, I take it you're interested in her and wonder why she hasn't looked at you. My response to that is that you're a closed-minded cynical person who if he doesn't get his way makes everyone else pay. She wants someone who complements her, not suppresses or hinders her. I have no problem telling you that I love her and you definitely don't. You have to be able to look outside yourself to love a woman like that. And you, sir—I don't believe you even know how to go about it."

Trent has a look of fire in his eyes and glares at Bryce. It's as though he's about to snap in seconds. Bryce notices it out of the corner of his eye and braces himself silently. Trent has no clue who he is messing with and thinks he can take Bryce.

"*Cynical!!* My ass! Man, you're a pompous asshole! What, you came to our band because no else would take you! You have all these ideas, but my question is why haven't you made it yet? You ain't nothing, and it's only a matter of time before Omani figures it out!" Trent replies.

Bryce stops the car by the side of the road, almost hitting a skater. He looks at Trent very intensely, ready to defend himself with whatever means necessary. He sits there clenching his fists, ready to fight. Trent looks back at him with his upper lip twitching.

"If you had done your homework you would have found out that I was in a major band. But two band members died in a fatal car accident, so we disbanded," Bryce starts to explain. He opens up a CD case and pulls one out and throws it at Trent. "Here's our CD. Now I suggest if you want this fucking tattoo you'll either shut up or get the hell out of my car. If you want to get physical I'm game. But you'd just better hope that you'll like your new face. Now, which will it be?"

Trent looks at the CD. On the cover is Bryce standing beside the other members of a well-known band. He starts to turn red in the face from the embarrassment. He doesn't even have the strength to look Bryce in the eye. He just keeps staring at the CD. Bryce doesn't take his eyes off of him for a second. In fact, he is waiting for an answer, clenching his fists and tapping a foot, shaking with adrenaline. Trent begins to tremble as he feels Bryce's intensifying anger building by the second. He turns his eyes slowly to Bryce without turning his face. He can tell that Bryce is ready to take him out. He gently puts the CD down and swallows hard.

"I didn't know," Trent replies.

"Yeah, well there's a lot you don't know. So instead of blabbing your mouth you need to listen and do your homework. Because next time there won't be a discussion. Got it?" Bryce says.

He unclenches his fists and puts the car in drive. Trent takes a deep breath, sitting back and closing his eyes and knowing that he will live to see another day. He then readjusts himself in the seat and remains quiet, looking out the window. Bryce turns up the music and begins to tap his fingers to the beat.

After driving for another fifteen minutes they stop outside a little shop. The building doesn't look very big, but there are a lot of cars parked around it. Trent doesn't say a word and just follows Bryce. They walk in and immediately see pictures everywhere of people exposing arms, legs, bellies, and backs. Trent just stands in the middle of the place staring at the pictures. Bryce shakes his head and snickers slightly at Trent's fascination. They can hear a machine not far away. A lady comes out from the back room and instantly smiles.

"Bryce, you're back!" she says, walking right up to him.

They touch fists, laughing. Bryce notices her arms and hands. Trent is still staring at the walls.

"I see you've decorated yourself since last time," he replies.

"Yeah, well, you know. So you here for a new tattoo?" she asks while showing off her new look. She has about eight tattoos and multiple piercings. She's wearing a tight outfit showing more skin that hiding it. Her hair is adventurous looking. It is obvious from her flirty yet slightly shy behavior that she has a crush on Bryce.

"No. Actually I brought a band member. He's interested in a tattoo. Just go easy on him. It's his first time. Hey, Trent, come here!!" he says.

Trent snaps out of it but looks dazed as he walks toward Bryce.

"A virgin, huh?" she says, and they both start laughing.

Bryce looks at Trent and notices the dazed look.

"They're going to take good care of you. Relax," he states, winking at the lady.

"Absolutely. You know what you want?" she asks.

"Yeah … I was uhh … thinking maybe a dragon here on my arm spitting fire and playing the drums. Here; I drew a something to give you an idea," he replies.

She smiles at his inexperienced drawing abilities, thinking it's cute. She turns around and walks to the desk and leans over, pulling out a book, and goes back to where they are standing.

"Dragons are a popular choice. Here are some examples; you know, to help with the picture. It will give you a more clear view," she says, handing the book to him.

Trent grabs the book and looks it over. The dragons are very well drawn and eye-catching. He lifts his head, thinking about which one would be perfect on his arm. Then something catches his eyes off to the side. There is a towel with very small needles on it. Trent's mouth falls open. He swallows and gives a nervous smile to Bryce, who is staring at the pictures in the book. As he continues looking at the needles, in his mind they keep getting larger by the second. Bryce notices Trent starting to sway yet standing still. He looks in the direction that has so much of Trent's attention and chuckles. When he turns back around, he notices Trent starting to lose color in his face. Bryce knows that the poor guy is about to go down. So thinking quickly he gets a chair from the nearby desk and places it by his knees and assists him in sitting down. The lady comes back over, seeing Trent in this altered state. She quickly grabs a glass of water from the huge five-gallon dispenser and hands it to him. Then she looks at Bryce, shrugging her shoulders and smiling.

"I've got a different idea," Bryce says.

Meanwhile, Omani and Amber are at a shopping center looking at clothes. They are in a hip store that carries a lot of cool items for people in the rock 'n' roll or hip-hop area. Almost immediately Omani is drawn to one area of the store and walks straight to it. Amber is still up front checking out the deals. Omani starts picking out clothes and goes to the dressing room. She puts on one outfit and comes out to the three-way mirrors located at the end of the dressing area. She has on a pair of jeans with leather accents and a very sexy top. She gets excited and then goes back to try on a few more outfits and comes out to look at them. Again, she is excited. This time she has on a dress with a funky sexy style, but it's similar to one she already owns. As she stares at herself the big smile quickly leaves. Omani suddenly starts thinking about what Bryce had said. It echoes in her mind. She realizes that the outfits aren't expressive enough. She goes back to the dressing room and comes back out with her normal clothes on. Looking disconcerted, Omani goes back to the area where the outfits are located and starts strategizing.

"What am I feeling that I want people to know?" she asks herself, thumbing through the clothes. While she's in deep thought, Amber comes over with an outfit.

"What do you think?" she asks.

Omani snaps out of it for a second and looks at the outfit. She frowns and shakes her head no.

"Remember, we need to express ourselves. You know, this is a lot harder than I thought. Bryce makes it look so easy," Omani replies, feeling defeated.

Then something on the wall catches her eyes. She is drawn to it and walks in that direction. Amber is talking but then notices her sister walking away. Amber turns around, looking in her sister's direction and trying to figure out what's going on. When Omani stops, Amber catches up to her.

"It's perfect. It may need a little tweaking, but it will work. And look, there's one in a different style for you. I think I know what I want to do," Omani replies, giving a flirtatious devilish grin.

An hour later Omani and Amber are rushing to the car as fast as possible with bags in their hands.

"Come on; we're going to be late," Omani says, throwing the bags in the car.

Before Amber can close the car door, Omani starts it up and begins driving. They dash off quickly, swerving past cars to get on the highway. Amber looks at her watch, noticing that they only have ten minutes before everyone meets.

"I know Trent. If we're too late, he'll leave and come back and throw a fit for an hour. Then we get nowhere but have to listen to him complain. Then I have to give him a huge lecture and so on. We don't have time for that today. Crap! Look at this; we're never going to get there in time. I'm taking the shortcut," Omani says.

She does a hard right. Amber holds onto the door handle almost in fear for her life.

"Slow down. Remember that Trent is with Bryce. Plus, neither one of us is going to put up with his crap today. This is too important. And we need to get there in one piece, don't you think?" Amber says.

"You're right," Omani says, slowing down and driving more safely.

They each take a deep breath, not looking at the time any more. They start laughing and carrying on about various things. Then suddenly out of nowhere something comes straight at the car. It's very dark and moving at lightning speed. Omani is laughing and turns her head from looking at Amber back to the road. She sees a glimpse of the thing coming straight for the car and swerves to the side of the road. Amber screams, and the car careens back and forth. Omani has both hands on the steering wheel while placing her foot on the brake. They come to a sudden stop.

"What the hell was that?" Amber asks.

"I don't know. But whatever it is isn't good," Omani replies, looking around in all directions. Amber is looking out her window. Neither one sees anything. They look at each other with fright in their eyes, and Omani starts driving again. Then they hear a strange loud knocking noise. It stops for a second but then comes back somewhere else, sounding even more weird.

"What's happening?" Amber asks.

"I don't know. Hold on. Do you have the stuff? I think we need it," Omani says, speeding up.

"No! I forgot it," Amber answers.

Nothing can be seen on the road in front of them or beside them. So Omani looks up at the rearview mirror and sees those red vicious eyes inside it. They jump out and dash at Omani and then go past her. She screams, swerving the car again.

"There's something in the car. I can feel it. But it's not really here. It's like it's somewhere else. You know, like transmitting itself from another destination but it still has a lot of strength. I don't know how to describe it," Amber says.

Then they hear a taunting low voice.

"You can't stop us. The power is too strong for you, bitch!" it says.

"Did you just hear that?" Omani asks.

"Yeah!" she replies.

The car stalls.

"Come on; get out," Omani says, opening the door.

The thing starts to laugh with an evil bone-shaking sound. It has both the ladies' attention as it floats up in the air and then quickly disappears. The sisters look at each other, horrified and not knowing what to think. Then the red eyes appear from behind Amber and dash toward Omani.

"Look out!" Omani screams.

Amber ducks but is unable to see what is there. She looks around, trying to figure out what's happening.

"What is it?" Amber asks.

"Those eyes," Omani replies.

They swoop close to Omani's face, showing the deep emotion of hate. She stands there frozen in fear; then they disappear.

"Is this what Grandma was warning me about? If so, I think we're in trouble," Omani says.

"What are we going to do?" Amber asks.

"We need to focus. It's just trying to scare us. I'm not going to let this thing win. We need Bryce. Come on," Omani replies.

They get back in the car. Omani starts it up and places her trembling right foot on the accelerator. They speed off, leaving a mark on the road.

CHAPTER 12

GABE, BRYCE, AND TRENT are sitting around talking and carrying on about the tattoo experience. They all can't help but laugh at it all. While laughing, Trent looks at his watch, secretly noticing the time. They are at the ladies' house sitting in the living room. Jasper is rubbing against their legs and purring. Trent starts sneezing. Gabe walks over to Bryce, who is showing off his various tattoos. The other two are quite impressed with them. Gabe asks several questions out of curiosity but has no intent of doing anything like that himself. Gabe has an even greater fear of needles that Trent does, but no one knows it. While they are absorbed in this great discussion, the front door quickly opens, slamming into the wall. The ladies can't get in fast enough carrying the bags of clothes. They stumble over each other. The door remains open as they go into the living room and see everyone sitting there. Bryce turns around, smiling. The ladies are trying to say hello but are out of breath with panicked looks on their faces. They put their bags down, trying to get it together.

"Hey, you're late," Trent says, holding up his arm with the watch pointing in their direction.

The ladies ignore him, looking serious. Time is the last thing on their minds.

"Bryce, can I talk to you please?" Omani says, walking toward the kitchen while trying to come across cool, calm, and collected.

Gabe and Trent look at each other, shrugging their shoulders. Omani had sounded somewhat stern. Trent turns away, giving a queasy smile. He thinks Omani is going to break up with Bryce or at least give a tongue lashing. Trent sits back all content waiting for a somber man to come out of the kitchen. Bryce rushes into the kitchen behind Omani. He is full of curiosity and concern. He slicks his hair back, diligently looking at Omani and trying to think of a way to remain cool. He's not sure what to make of the situation.

"What is it?" he asks.

"We were attacked," Amber replies.

"*What?* Are you okay?" he says, shocked, and rushes to her side.

"We're fine. I don't know if it was the spirit Grandma warned me about or not. But we really don't have much time," Omani says.

Bryce is obviously upset and begins to fidget, but he tries to cover it up by appearing in problem-solving mode. He rubs two fingers over his bottom lip.

"Okay, let's do this thing with the band that we planned. Then we need to start figuring out where Zadku's Point is located. Just stay cool and keep it together. We can do this. Come on," Bryce says, trying to keep everyone afloat. Amber nods her head and walks out of the kitchen. Bryce goes up to Omani and holds her close. She leans into him, releasing all her tension by resting her head on his shoulders.

"Why do you make me feel so safe?" she whispers to him.

He kisses her on the cheek. "I take it you've got an outfit?" he whispers softly in return.

She nods in confirmation and rubs his chest while smiling. Then he softly turns her head in his direction and kisses her on the lips intensely but softly. Bryce brushes her cheek and smiles. They can hear loud laughing in the other room, so he takes her by the hand and walks her out to the living room.

"Hey, everyone, they got the outfits!" Bryce says happily.

They all shout in excitement. Trent hides his disappointment at seeing the two still together with a distant smile.

"Hey, Omani, Amber, you've got to see Trent's tattoo!" Gabe says.

"You did it?" Amber replies, shocked and amazed.

"Not exactly. But close enough. Take a look," Bryce says.

The ladies go over to Trent to look at his right arm. There sits a dragon playing the drums with fire spitting out of its mouth. Omani puts her hand over his tattoo.

"It feels different. Not like yours," she says to Bryce.

"Well, they couldn't do the tattoo today because they were missing a specific color. So he had a paint job done instead. In the future he can get the actual one. But for now this will do," Bryce says, giving Trent a look that his secret is safe. Trent looks at Bryce with shock and admiration after all that had happened earlier.

The group forms a circle and gets down to business. They discuss the looks for the show and how to stand out after seeing that striking drawing. Gabe and Trent plan on wearing something black with a color twist. Bryce has an outfit that brought him luck in the last band that he plans on wearing. But he doesn't want to spoil the surprise of what it looks like yet. The ladies picked out something they want to surprise everyone with too. They hold up the bag, teasing everyone. The excitement builds in the air. They all stand up, placing their hands in the center and saying how committed they are to making this real. They stay in the circle for a second.

"Okay, tomorrow we'll do a practice round before the real thing. Let's not just do a performance; let's make history!" Omani says.

The whole group shouts in excitement and anticipation. Although they wanted to practice right away, there are more important things to do.

"I say we save our energy for tomorrow and sleep good tonight. See everyone tomorrow," Omani says.

The group all does their happy good-byes, looking to a bright future. Trent makes a point to approach Bryce quickly and privately right before leaving.

"Hey, thanks. You're all right," Trent whispers.

Bryce nods, feeling that the tension between them is now gone. He helps Trent and Gabe by taking their equipment out to their cars. As soon as the front door closes, Omani and Amber look at each other, knowing what the other is thinking without speaking. They make a mad dash for the stairs and enter the back bedroom and open the cedar chest. They quickly start thumbing through some readings, leaving their clothes and musical apparatus out downstairs. Bryce comes back in, not seeing them anywhere in sight. He can hear them talking and heads up the stairs. Jasper follows him, staying close to his side and almost causing him to trip. Upon entering the door, he sees the girls frantically looking for any clues to Zadku's Point. There are papers scattered all over the floor, which isn't helpful. Bryce goes up to them and grabs the papers out of their hands. They turn around and look at him, speechless, wondering what's up.

"What are you doing?" Omani asks.

"You're not going to find it like that," he replies.

"How do you know?" Amber asks.

"Because that's why your Grandma came to her. It's a special place for a reason, and it can't fall into the wrong hands. It's time to think outside of the box. Here," he says, handing a white candle to Omani.

She looks at it, thrown for a loop. She's wondering if it's some part of a joke.

"What's with this?" she asks.

"You can see the future, right? That's what you need. While you're setting up, I'm going to experiment. When you're ready I'll bring the granny glasses in," he replies, putting on the glasses and smiling. He winks and then turns around and walks out of the room.

"Well, this ought to be interesting," Amber says.

"Well, it's my power. I just have to figure out how to get it to work. Got a match?" Omani replies.

The ladies head downstairs to the kitchen where there's a small breakfast bar. Omani places the candle in the center with nothing around it. Then she grabs a chair. Amber lights the candle and sits down quietly, away from her sister; she doesn't want to break her concentration. Omani pulls up the chair and stares at the candle, hoping something will happen. Nothing does. All she sees is the smoke going up into the air. She slaps her hands on her thighs out of frustration. After a few minutes, Omani closes her eyes for a while and then opens them. Still nothing. She sighs. Frustrated, she readjusts herself in the chair and holds her hands out in the air.

"Bring what is the unknown for the future to the known. Guide it through the light so my eyes can see," Omani says.

She focuses on the candle again, looking so hard at the candle that the flames seem to disappear.

"Anything?" Amber quietly asks.

Omani slumps a little in disappointment and turns to her sister.

"Nothing. But I've got to keep trying. Oh that's right; I need those glasses. Dang it, where's Bryce?" she replies.

Meanwhile, Bryce is walking slowly and carefully around the house. He looks at everything, trying to spot if anything is out of the ordinary. Everything seems to be in its place. Jasper is still by his side and starts to meow. He looks down at the cat.

"Don't they ever feed you?" he asks.

They cat meows even louder, looking at Bryce in the face. Bryce reaches down and pets him, hoping that will get him to be quiet. When he stands back up, he sees what looks like a person standing there. He is shocked and jumps back, realizing it's some type of spirit.

"Sorry, didn't see you there," he says.

The spirit is in a brown monk robe with a hood that hides the face and has long sleeves with checks and balance symbols at the end of it. A finger appears with a strange glow pointing to a specific area of the house. Bryce tries to figure out what this thing is pointing toward. He gets nowhere.

"I didn't quite get that. Want to try again?" he asks.

Bryce has the rods in his hands. They start to sway back and forth. He looks down at them, startled by the movement, and holds them out in front of him. One of the rods keeps swaying while the other seems to move about differently. He doesn't know what to make of it, so he holds out his fingers so that he is barely touching them. Bryce is trying to make sure he's not the one moving them. After a few seconds he figures out that it's not him. It actually seems to spook the guy a little. Suddenly one rod stops doing the strange movements and actually ventures off to one direction and stays there. Bryce gets it to come back to the original spot. But then it moves again, pointing to the same area. The other rod just sways. He looks off in the direction where the rod is pointing. There's a family picture on the wall above the fireplace. He looks back at the spirit. It also points in that direction.

"I take it you want me to go this way," he says.

Bryce walks over to the picture, trying to figure out the significance. There's nothing the visible eye can see that is out of the ordinary. So he puts down the rods and carefully looks behind the picture. There's nothing there. He looks on the back of the painting and then feels it. Everything is normal. Bryce then looks at the top of the mantel to see if anything sticks out. There's nothing unusual. He looks down on the floor. Still nothing. He picks up the rods again. This time they both move in a direction and stop, pointing off to the side of the fireplace. He turns his head away from the fireplace to look at the spirit, thinking it is still across the room. But instead it is almost in his face.

"Oh, hello," he says, taking a step back. "You wouldn't want to show yourself, would you?"

The spirit just points again.

"Didn't think so," he replies.

Bryce goes to where the rods are pointing. Again there's nothing out of the ordinary. Then Jasper comes up to him and starts meowing again.

"What is your problem?" he asks.

He reaches down to pet the cat again. Suddenly he sees a discolored brick that stands out from the rest next to the fireplace. He kneels down and carefully takes the brick from its place. Inside is a small hole where there looks to be a piece of paper stashed. He takes it out and turns around carefully, not knowing where the spirit may be standing; but it is gone. Bryce unravels the piece of paper. The ink is faded, but when he holds up to the light he starts to see something.

"Oh shit! She needs the glasses," he says.

Bryce places the paper in his pocket and dashes off to the kitchen. He carefully opens the door and tiptoes into the room. Neither lady notices him as he quietly places the glasses next to Omani. Bryce winks and walks back out, heading for the stairs.

Meanwhile, Omani gets up from her chair, suddenly noticing the glasses. She is taken aback and looks around for Bryce, wondering how he did that without being noticed. But time is wasting, so she puts the glasses on.

"I sure hope this works, because I'm exhausted," she says.

"Yeah, I'm tired too. In fact, I think I want to lie down," Amber says, getting up. She hits the light switch out of force of habit.

"Oops, I'm sorry," Amber says, about to turn it back on.

"No, don't worry about it. I already feel like I'm in the dark anyway. I'll just blow out the candle and be up after this try," Omani says, sighing.

Amber leaves the room. Omani turns around, feeling like a failure and hopelessly pushing the glasses closer to her eyes. She looks at the candle, and suddenly images appear in the air above it, taking her by surprise. She stands there in awe as the images start to slowly become more clear. She is so taken by the mystique of it that when she tries to sit in the chair she almost misses it but catches herself. She grabs the seat as she begins to sit. The images are going around in a circular fashion. Then the motion starts to slow a little, and one image becomes more bold and colorful. It actually jumps out toward her, beginning to show

106

up more clearly. It looks like a rocky place that is peaceful, but the colors around it are red and a strange yellow. It's like a warning sign amid the peacefulness. Then the image changes. It shows a stone stairway with strange writing on the walls. It looks ancient. Then it shows people at the top of the stairs in the middle of something indescribable. As Omani focuses closely on the image, she realizes that the people are the three of them. But there is something dark and nasty coming from behind them. Suddenly the image disappears.

"Wait. Come back. Crap, that didn't help much," Omani says, feeling even more confused.

Then the kitchen lights are turned on.

"What didn't help?" Bryce asks, walking in with the paper in his hand.

Omani is about to answer but is too frustrated. Bryce gets closer to her, feeling her hesitation and frustration.

"Did you see anything?" he asks in a low-key seductive voice.

She takes a deep breath and sighs.

"Yes, but it didn't really tell me anything. I think it tried to show me somewhere ancient," she replies, slightly discouraged.

"Oh well, then maybe this will help," he says, grabbing a chair and coming over to where she is sitting.

"You found something?" she says, feeling renewed with hope.

He unfolds the paper again and holds it up to the light. Then he moves it around a bit trying to get the light to shine on it just right.

"There; do you see it?" he asks with excitement.

Omani gets in real close trying to look in exactly the same area as Bryce.

"No. What is it?" she asks.

He repositions himself in the chair so that she can get a better view. He tweaks the position of the paper while also watching the expression on Omani's face. Suddenly her eyes light up.

"Whoa! What was that?" she says.

He stops moving the paper while Omani stands up to get a closer look.

"What is it?" she asks.

"I think it's a map," he replies.

She looks at it even more closely.

"There. I saw those ancient-looking drawings in the vision. I've never seen anything like that before; have you?" she asks.

"No, but it's time to find out," he says.

They head into the living area where the computer is located and sit down. Omani brings up the screen and types in "ancient cultures" to see what comes up. She sees a whole bunch of choices and then changes the search to "ancient writings." She gets even fewer choices. She starts clicking on the different ones to see what happens. Nothing stands out.

"Click on that one," Bryce says.

Omani clicks on one that is off to the side. It takes a second to download. Then at the top of the page she sees one of the pictures she saw in the vision.

"Hey, I saw that in the vision," Omani says, scrolling down.

They read the page together. As they scroll down a little more they see more symbols. Then it talks about a location.

"It says here that it is in the desert. It's a lost culture most don't know anything about. I think I know where it is," Bryce replies.

Omani turns and looks at him, mesmerized.

"Where?" she asks.

"After tomorrow, I'll show you. But I have a feeling we won't be alone. We need to be prepared. We need to practice our powers together first," he says.

"What's so special about Zadku's Point? I know that's where I receive the power of Vuex. But why there?" she asks.

"I don't know. But I have a feeling we're about to find out. As far as tonight goes, I say we start that date. What do you think?" he says.

Omani is about to say something, but Bryce places his finger on her lips to get her to stop.

"No questions; remember? Come with me," he replies in a sexy whisper.

He takes her by the hand and guides her upstairs quietly so as not to disturb Amber. She is very curious as to what he has planned, but she just smiles and goes along with it. He leads her into the big bathroom where there are several candles lit and bathwater with bubbles. There are two glasses with a wine bottle next them. She is almost in tears when she sees it all. He quietly closes the door and holds her in his arms.

"I thought we could enjoy a little bubbly in the tubly," he says very seductively.

He slowly removes his clothes, never taking his eyes off of her. Omani's breath is taken away. Then Bryce gets close to her and begins to disrobe her while caressing her skin and surrounding her with a large towel. They look deep into each others' eyes. He wraps his arms around her, and they start kissing. He walks her slowly to the tub and guides her in. Right before sitting, she throws the towel aside and sits close to this romantic man. He gently begins touching her while kissing her softly and gently. He holds her head next to his chest while giving a gentle massage. Omani listens to his heart beating with both eyes closed. He notices her starting to fall sleep, so Bryce wraps his legs around her while starting the jets. She wakes up laughing. They kiss in a playful manner, enjoying each other. Bryce leans over a little and picks up the two glasses of wine. They say, "Cheers," kissing each other. After a few sips, he takes both glasses and sets them back down. Bryce looks at Omani with deep and love admiration and positions himself in a way to give her a very passionate kiss. The kiss is so intense that it leaves Omani speechless and desiring more. With no words spoken, he guides her out of the tub wrapped in a towel and leads her to the bedroom. Candles are lit in there too, with a dozen roses lying on the bed. He lays her down, gazing into her eyes. They begin making very passionate love. They are so engrossed in each other that a bomb could have gone off and neither one would have heard it. Omani looks at the ceiling and smiles. For the first time, she's is in love, and her face is glowing with it.

CHAPTER 13

LATE IN THE MORNING Amber comes down the stairs yawning in some comfortable sleeping clothes. She can hear Bryce and Omani talking in the kitchen. She stops at the foot of the stairs to listen. It sounds intense, almost like an argument, but it's a discussion. She starts walking, cautiously looking into the living room. Jasper is staring at the wall, flopping his tail with those cute ears pinned back. Amber's eyes move around, quickly trying to figure out what's going on. She hesitantly walks to the kitchen and slowly opens the door. Bryce and Omani are sitting at the breakfast bar having eggs, toast, and coffee while in deep discussion. She tries to get a glimpse of what is happening, but before she knows it Omani turns her head and sees her.

"Great. You're just in time," Omani says.

Amber slowly opens the door the rest of the way. Bryce turns around, holding some strange papers in his hands.

"What's going on?" Amber asks.

"We were just talking about where we think Zadku's Point is located. After you went upstairs last night, the candle worked and showed me something. We're looking on the computer trying to figure out where it is," Omani responds.

"You mean it actually worked?" Amber asks.

"Yep. It didn't help much. In fact, I think it may have caused some more confusion. I think it's somewhere ancient, and he thinks it's out in the middle of nowhere in the desert. I think we can use a break," Omani says.

"What's that?" Amber asks, looking in Bryce's hand.

He looks down at his hand and then looks up again and smiles.

"This is a map. When it's in the right light it seems to show something. But I can't quite make it out. Want to try?" Bryce asks, holding it out to Amber.

She approaches and grabs the paper, quickly holding it up to the light to try to see anything. Then she suddenly puts the paper down to her side and looks at Omani. Amber has had a revelation. Omani knows that something is up and turns around, noticing the look.

"What's the matter?" Omani asks.

"This paper. Do you remember when we were kids when Grandma used this paper with us? But in order for the picture to show up she would hand us something. Remember?" Amber replies.

Omani stands there thinking really hard and trying to recall. She has one hand on her hip and the other by the sink looking down. Then her eyes enlarge and she looks at Amber.

"That's right! It was that strange pumice mixed with something else that stunk. Ugh!! I can still smell it after all these years. But wait! I think I know where there is some. She gave me some and made me promise to keep it. Come on," Omani states, taking off running. Bryce and Amber follow. They go downstairs where there is an old stained wooden cupboard area. It looks very old and like it could fall apart at any time. Omani slowly and carefully opens the cabinet door. It creaks loudly, and the whole thing shakes like it's going to crumble. Amber stands back with her hands out ready to catch any pieces that might fall. Bryce is intrigued by the cabinet and looks it over, admiring the old craftsmanship. Omani pulls out a small sealed plastic container. She takes it away from the cabinet area and takes off the tape surrounding the lid. Then she takes the lid off. It makes a popping noise from being sealed for so long. A small cloud of smoke comes out.

"*Ugh!!* That smell!" Omani says, turning away and holding her arm fully extended.

Amber comes over to reach into the container.

"Wait! I have rubber gloves over there by the washer," Omani says, pointing with her chin.

Bryce goes over and picks up the gloves while she brings the container over to the washer. Omani shuts the washer lid and places the container on top. Bryce opens the map again and sets it down and puts on the gloves. He reaches into the container and pulls out a strange-looking pumice rock. It looks purple with orange-red pores, almost looks like it's from a different planet.

"Okay, what am I supposed to do?" Bryce asks.

Omani gets a little closer, keeping her face clear of the stuff.

"You gently rub the pumice over the paper and then place it in a dark spot for about five minutes. Then look at it," Omani replies.

Bryce does just that and then places the stuff back into the container, sealing it. Omani closes it back in the cabinet. Bryce and Amber look around, trying to find a dark place, but there are little glimpses of sunlight everywhere. While both ladies are busy, the dryer door opens. They both turn around, noticing Bryce putting the paper in there and closing the door.

"So how am I going to dry my clothes now? That stuff will stink anything up for eternity. Thanks, Bryce," Omani says.

He smiles, watching and not taking his eyes off the wrist watch.

"I always enjoy a wet T-shirt contest," he replies with a huge grin.

Omani squints her eyes at him, reacting to the flirtatious behavior. After five minutes he pulls out the paper and races upstairs. The ladies can't keep up with him because he so quick. With high anticipation he goes into the living room where the sun is shining the strongest and looks the paper over closely. A whole different image appears. There are symbols of what looks like an ancient culture.

"What is this?" he says, puzzled by the finding.

Omani and Amber take a closer look. They see a funky-looking hill that has a little bit of a pyramid shape.

"*That's what I saw!*" Omani screams, taking a step back.

"Okay," Bryce replies, looking it over. "I've seen these symbols before. I think it's ancient Greek. Check it out. I know two of the symbols. This one means trail, and this one means to enter from the back. I'm not sure about the other four. I'll have to do some research."

Omani is getting a little nervous and roams silently in the living area, thinking.

"Okay, before we go any further I think we need to strengthen our powers and learn how to work together as a team. Otherwise, I'm not sure if we can handle Zadku's Point," Omani says.

"She's right," Amber replies.

"Okay. So how are we going to do that?" Bryce asks.

They all think for a second, looking around for any sign of inspiration. The place is so completely quiet that one could hear a pin drop. Jasper is even quietly watching everyone from a corner. Every second the ticks from the clock in the living room seem to get louder and louder as the intensity in the room increases.

"I know," Omani says, shocking everyone, even the cat. "We need to go where there is a lot of negativity. Because where's there's negativity there are nasty spirits we can practice on. But we need to go where it's not too strong."

"How about a different graveyard?" Amber says.

"No. They figured out that we go there. But I've got it—a hospital," Omani replies.

Bryce and Amber look at Omani like she has just flipped her lid. This spirit stuff is starting to go a little haywire. Noticing the looks on their faces, she places her hands on her hips. Her stern look could pierce their skin like a needle.

"Think about it! There's death and dying. Those things hang around that, right?" she replies.

Bryce nods his head.

"Okay, when?" he asks.

"Tonight after practice," Omani replies.

"*Tonight?* How are we going to have enough time for all of this? Tomorrow is the big day for the band, remember?" Amber replies.

"We're going to have to make it work, or we may be dealing with another power outage while performing," Omani responds.

"The power goes out?" he asks.

"Yeah. It did the first night all this crap happened," Amber replies.

Bryce thinks deeply, silently nodding his head. An idea comes across his mind along with a contented smile.

"I'll meet you guys there. I'm going to run an errand," he says.

Later in the evening the band is at the venue where they're going to perform the next night in front of the agents. Everybody is setting up their equipment. Trent is preparing the speakers to start doing sound checks. He places a microphone in front of the keyboard, and Gabe turns it on. Trent starts wandering around, listening to see how everything sounds. When there is an issue, which there always is with him, he lets the bar manager know. That way the necessary changes can be made. With his perfectionist attitude setting up can sometimes be a painstaking experience. Overall, it takes about an hour for them to finish. They come down to the floor and grab chairs, facing each other. The tension and excitement is so thick it could be cut with a knife. Everybody has their own nervous twitches, and they all are exposing them at this point in time. It's different to dream something than to bring it to reality. For them this dream means everything, but will others see it the same way? They all can't help but think about what they're going to do if this doesn't work out. The nervous twitches have them all on edge, but everybody is trying very hard to keep their cool.

"Okay, I know the show is tomorrow night, but I want us to pretend it's tonight. I want to rock this place. If anybody messes up, I want us to just go on like it's the real deal. This is what we've been waiting for, so let's do it!" Omani says, inspiring everybody.

Everybody puts their hands in and shouts the band's name loud and clear. Then Bryce gets up and dashes toward the bar. Everybody wonders what's wrong. When he returns the owner follows with a tray of shots.

"Thought we all deserved a round," Bryce says.

Everybody stands back up, holding a shot in the air.

"For the band; may this be the beginning of our future!" Bryce says and then swallows.

Then everybody else swallows. They put the empty shot glasses back on the tray, and the owner takes it away. They head up to the stage like it was the actual day of the show. The rush feeling among the band members starts to kick in, keeping their spirits high, and they begin to play. Before anybody really gets a chance to start their instruments, Bryce roars his guitar. It is electrifying. Nobody in the band frowns. In fact, it gives them the inspiration to rise to the occasion. They all begin rocking and playing like never before, making the manager stop his work duties to watch. Omani and Amber sing with such grace that it brings everything together. Omani is so into it that her eyes are closed, focusing completely on the music along with the feeling. Bryce can't take his eyes off of her. In fact, it is making him so desirous toward her that the chords on the guitar express the emotion vividly. People start coming in from the outside knowing the place isn't open but wanting to watch. The owner tries to escort them back out. But suddenly what started with just a few people is now a line beginning to form. Within ten minutes half the place is packed. The owner shrugs his shoulders and decides to flip on the dim lights while opening the bar. When the band finishes, people are whistling, shouting, and screaming for more. Omani opens her eyes to the noise, surprised to see all the people there. She looks at the band and just smiles. They all stand still in their spots, feeling very pleased with the performance. Omani grabs the microphone.

"Thank you, everyone!! Wow! Your support is so appreciated!! If you liked this, please come tomorrow night for a spectacular concert," Omani states.

"You won't be disappointed!" Amber adds. The group comes together and goes to the back behind the bar. They are giggling with excitement.

"Wow!! Did you see all those people?" Amber says.

"We're going to do it. I know it!" Trent says.

"That is the most positive thing I've heard from you in a long time!! I think with that we all get another round of drinks. What do you say?" Omani replies.

They all go back out to the front, signaling the manager to bring them drinks. Bryce puts his arms around Omani and kisses her. Gabe smiles at his girlfriend and then gives her a quick kiss. When the drinks come, they all hug with one hand in a circle and drink with the other. They scream the band name again.

"I have to say that was impressive," Bryce states.

"I can see that record deal now," Gabe replies.

After they all calm down from the excitement, the group goes over simple changes for tomorrow night. Then they wrap it up. In the back there is a small storage area that the manager set aside for them to put some of the equipment, and they place anything of value there. When they have all finished, the manager rattles the keys in his hands after escorting out the last customer.

"Well, time to lock up. I hope tomorrow night goes as well," he says.

They thank him and head out toward their cars. Trent and Gabe get into a separate car since they can't all six fit in one. The others climb into the other. They wave at each other while driving away.

"What a fantastic night!" Amber says.

Omani sighs. "Yeah. Unfortunately we have to end it with a not-so-fantastic time. The hospital is right up there, Bryce," she comments, pointing.

"Yes, but remember that the goal is only to strengthen our powers," Bryce says.

"Yeah, well, tell that to the spirits," Omani says.

Bryce pulls up to the hospital and shuts off the engine; the headlights go out. They get out of the car just looking around the hospital parking lot. As a group they move slowly toward the hospital, trying to be tuned into whatever may be around. Amber is carrying the duffle bag, and Bryce has the book and various papers. Omani is carrying a camera. As they approach the front of the hospital the doors open, but there is no one around the main area.

"This is kind of eerie, isn't it?" Amber states.

"Just come on. Let's get this over with, and fast," Omani replies, walking toward the exit sign near the end of the hallway.

She pushes open the door and goes down the stairs.

"Where are we going?" Bryce asks.

"The morgue," Omani replies.

Amber stops in the process of going down the stairs.

"Where?" she asks.

"You guys, we don't have much time. If those negative things are at a cemetery, they're going to be at a morgue. *Now come on!*" Omani orders, preceding them down the stairs.

"Doesn't it concern you that your sister *knows* where the morgue is?" Bryce says.

"I heard that! And no, I don't. Logically speaking what hospital would have a morgue on the fifth floor? They are *always* in the basement," Omani says.

Bryce chuckles, enjoying teasing her when she is in a goal-oriented mood. Amber gives him a look to remind him to be careful because he is treading on thin ice. She knows not to make Omani mad when she's on a mission. When they hit the bottom of the stairs Omani looks around at various doors. Bryce and Amber just watch her, not knowing what's going on. Finally, she opens a door and walks in, disappearing for a second. She comes back out with three lab coats and quickly hands them to the others and proceeds down the hallway. They see a small sign in dark letters with the word "morgue" on it. There's an electronic keypad for access on the outside of the door. Omani takes a deep sigh and starts thinking. Then the door suddenly opens.

"I was wondering when you guys were getting here. I've been waiting for almost two hours," a man with thick glasses states. He is an older gentleman with grey hair and a small gut. Omani knows to think quickly on the feet or walk away.

"Sorry. There was a holdup. How can we be of great service to you?" she asks.

He starts walking back to his station where a half-eaten sandwich lies. There beside the eating area is also the working zone. The three of them frown upon noticing it and gag a little. There is a partially exposed corpse that has obviously already been worked on. The older gentleman takes a bite out of his sandwich and heads over to the body, which is only a few feet away, right near a sign stating no drinking or eating.

"Here is an approximately forty-year-old male who was found right outside the hospital. They're trying to figure out if there was foul play. I haven't noticed anything, but the way crimes are done these days you never know. That's why I called you guys. I bet you see a lot of interesting crime scenes. Anyway, while you're doing your thing, do you mind if I take a quick fifteen-minute break?" he asks.

"No. Go right on ahead," Bryce replies.

The guy wastes no time exiting the premises.

"Well, that was easy," Amber comments.

"Let's get started," Omani says, pointing at the duffel bag.

Amber opens the bag and takes out the rods, a white candle, Grandma's glasses, and some writings. She places the candle by the sandwich and lights it. Bryce folds the glasses over the front of his T-shirt. They form a circle and face each other.

"Everybody close your eyes and focus. Let's feed off each others' energy and let things happen. It may take a while," Omani says.

"Hopefully not longer than fifteen minutes," Bryce says.

They close their eyes and place their hands up in the air at waist height so that they are touching. The first few minutes there is nothing but silence. They can hear each other breathing. It's almost hypnotic. Every few seconds Amber opens her eyes just to make sure nothing in the room has moved. Omani doesn't open her eyes but knows that something is up and squeezes her sister's hand hard. After a few more minutes everyone is in deep concentration.

"There's something here! It's in the left corner at the south wall. I can feel it," Amber says slowly while in concentration. Omani opens her eyes slowly, looking in that direction. A shadowy human figure appears.

"I can see it. Let me try to talk to it," Omani says.

They still have their hands in place with all their eyes closed again. As Omani tries to communicate with it, the figure creeps ever so slowly closer to the group.

"It's almost beside me," Amber says.

"I know. It's a man. He's trying to talk to me. Basically, what I'm getting is that he's trapped by someone or something," Omani responds.

"Something else just entered, and it's very negative. And powerful!" Amber replies with a tremble in the voice.

"Okay, it's time to break away. Amber, you get the rods. Omani, keep trying to talk to him. I'm going to put the glasses on," Bryce says.

They carefully break away from each other. Each goes to do their separate thing. Amber picks up the rods and notices them pointing in the direction of the negative being. Omani keeps her eyes closed, trying to keep the connection. Bryce places the glasses on and immediately sees the dead man and the nasty-looking entity. It has a nonhuman look to it, almost like a creature from outer space. It has a beast head and the body of a man. The man is crying, almost pleading.

"We're going to help you," Bryce says to him.

"Okay, he's stating that there's a negative being that is about to take him. There's a dark portal on the other side of that wall, and it's trying to pull him into it. The negative entity is very strong and will eventually pull him through and take him. This man is trapped by his own actions, and the guilt of it is heavy," Omani states, opening her eyes to look at the man.

"Whatever you did that you feel guilty about, let it go," Bryce says.

"He's telling me that he and others dabbled in the occult. The portal he opened has never been closed. Many entities have been coming through it, and nobody knows it. He has attempted to close it, but three men jumped him and then gave a blow to a hidden surgical site on his back. Afterwards, the man was left for dead. He regrets dabbling and says he was just experimenting, not realizing the consequences," Omani replies.

The negative force approaches the poor guy and starts pulling him to the portal. The man appears to be screaming and reaching out toward Bryce. He is frightened of what might happen and lifts his arms. Bryce runs toward the wall, holding out his hands. Suddenly a strange orange glow appears and shelters the man. The negative entity tries to break through but can't. It tries many times and fails. So it turns its attentions on Bryce and begins to approach him fiercely.

"The rods. *Now!!*" Bryce says.

Omani quickly turns around and holds onto the rods with Amber. Bryce opens the canister and sprinkles the dust. A portal appears. The entity has a terrified look on its face as it tries to fight back. But the rods pull it toward the portal. It slides through and disappears, and the portal closes. Then they all look toward the sad man. His tears stop, and the orange glow dissipates.

"He's saying thank you. But for him to go, the portal he opened must be closed. It's at the bar across the street," Omani says.

"Let's go before something else tries to take him," Bryce says.

They quickly gather their stuff and head for the door. The older man comes back, approaching the trio eating a candy bar.

"So what did you find out?" he asks.

"He was murdered. There's a surgical wound on the back where he was assaulted and killed," Omani replies.

"Wow; you guys really are good," he states.

The trio dash off out the door. The man takes a few bites out of his candy bar and then turns around to look at the group to talk more.

"Hey," he says, surprised to see them gone. He just shrugs his shoulders and closes the door.

CHAPTER 14

Across the street from the hospital a group of buildings is all lit up. At the end of the block is a building with an awning where people can pull up and get out of their car and go straight in. It looks very nice and prestigious from the outside. The other buildings don't have the awning feature but have more of a pub feel. As the trio approaches the group of nightclubs and bars they began to walk slowly, trying to pick up on any vibrations. They can hear loud music even though the doors are closed. People are coming and going all the time in each of the places. A few times the drunken people roaming about bump into the ladies. Bryce has to move them out of the way. When they are almost at the last building, they stop.

"I do too," Omani replies.

"What?" Bryce responds, puzzled by the remark.

Omani looks at him strangely.

"What?" she replies startled.

"You just said I do too," Bryce says.

"Yeah. I responded to Amber's comment about feeling something strange here," Omani replies, looking at Bryce like he's off his rocker.

"But I didn't say anything," Amber says.

They all look at each other, shocked.

"It worked. You communicated with Omani telepathically," Bryce replies, laughing and pleasantly surprised.

"We can celebrate that later because there's something very strange here. It's giving me the heebie-jeebies," Omani says.

"Your purse," Amber replies, staring at her.

Bryce turns his head to look at the purse too. It's swinging around in a circular fashion like a pendulum.

"I'm not doing it," Omani responds, shocked and horrified.

"I think we're close. Come on," Bryce says as he walks up to the door under the awning.

Upon entering the doorway, they see a guard standing there dressed very nicely in a suit wearing an earpiece . He places his hands out to stop them.

"ID please," he says, standing up strong, tough, and with intimidation.

They pull out their IDs and hand them to him. As soon as they flash them, they start to walk in. The guy stops them again.

"Do you have a reservation? This is an exclusive club," he replies.

Bryce stumbles over his words, trying to come up with something to say. The guard notices the stumped behavior and signals to the other guard to come and help escort them out.

"What are we going to do?" Amber says.

The guard looks Amber and Omani over closely.

"Aren't you in that band?" the other bouncer says, walking over with his eyes getting enlarged with every step.

"Yes," Omani responds.

"You guys are good!! Can I have your autograph?" he asks, all excited.

"Sure, if you let us in the club," Omani replies.

The guy nods his head and stops the others from approaching. The band members sign a napkin he has in front of him and proceed forward.

"Excellent thinking. Okay, let's split up and meet back there in that private-looking room," Bryce says.

They begin walking into the different areas of the place. There's a huge dance floor with a number of different levels. There are walkways to the side and some stairs to get to the next level. They each take a different direction, trying to pick up any vibration. The place is pretty crowded, which makes it difficult to work or move around. As they reach the back and meet up they each have a strong feeling of disappointment.

"Nothing," Amber replies.

"Me either," Omani replies.

"Now what? This is the place the vibe comes from," Bryce states, confused.

Omani's purse starts swinging like a pendulum again. The trio can't help but notice it. Suddenly the music stops, the lights go out, and the doors to the back slam shut. The people who are in the back room start screaming and running for any possible exit in sight. The trio stands still, listening to the panic. None of the doors will open. The frustration and anxiety build in the crowd.

"Oh goodie," Omani says.

A door off to the side opens slightly. The creaking noise attracts the people, and they run to it like a herd of cattle. Trying to squeeze through the tiny opening, in groups, makes the frustration even worse. People start pushing and shoving, all wanting to get through that small opening first.

"Well, isn't this entertaining?" Amber says.

"It doesn't want them. While they are leaving let's set up. I have feeling we're in for our own form of entertainment," Omani replies.

Amber pulls out a lighter and flicks it, waiting for a flame to develop. The group begins to set up everything in preparation for a fight.

"Do you see the pentagram anywhere?" Omani asks.

"Nope," Amber responds, looking around.

The last person squeezes through the door. After a few minutes the small crack remains open. They look at each other, bewildered, and shrug their shoulders in unison and walk toward the small opening. Suddenly it closes, and they can hear a strange whistling sound.

"I think we'd better hold onto something," Omani says, looking at a dancing pole within arm's length.

Bryce and Amber grab onto the bar area in the back. Omani reaches for the pole. But as she sticks out her arms, almost touching it, something forces her back. She is slammed into the wall hard. Things start flying around the room like there's a tornado.

"Omani, are you okay?" Bryce screams.

"It's got a hold of me. I can't move. Find the symbol!! That's our key!" she screams.

Bryce and Amber hold onto items while moving slowly and looking for the pentagram, but they find nothing. Amber opens up the container and throws the dust into the air. The portal appears for a second and then disappears.

"What happened?" Amber says, stunned.

"This thing is strong. It's going to take a lot more to get rid of it. Keep looking," Bryce screams.

Omani breaks away for a second and falls to the floor and starts crawling toward the bar area. Something grabs a hold and pulls her backward, dragging her across the floor. A strange red light from a corner of the room develops. It slowly gets larger and creeps toward Omani, developing into a demonic entity. Bryce and Amber are searching diligently for the symbol but have no luck. The walls start to turn slimy. A nasty stench fills the air, making them all start to gag. In the near distance they can see a bathroom door. Bryce points to it and heads in that direction. He's almost there when a nasty figure four times his size gets up in his face and screams. Bryce lets go due to its surprise. The whirlwind catches him and throws him up against the wall next to Omani.

"It's in the bathroom!" Bryce yells.

The strange red-glowing demon looks electrical and sparks as it touches the wall and approaches Bryce. He's terrified just by the look of it. Suddenly an orange glow appears around his body. The demonic presence with a beast head gets up close to him and is instantly detoured by the orange glow. It backs up and screams. Bryce and Omani stare at it, horrified. He realizes that it can't get through to him. It turns the attention on Omani and starts moving towards her. Bryce reaches for Omani's hand. It notices and tries to stop him, but Bryce beats the demon to her. An orange glow covers her too. The whirlwind continues but seems to go around them, and they're able to stand up.

"How did you do that?" Omani asks.

"Don't know. And I don't know how long it's going to last. Come on," he says.

They run to the bathroom. The door is closed tightly and will not budge. Bryce keeps pushing on it, getting nowhere. The negative presence is starting to come closer to them again. Something triggers Omani to close her eyes and point her head toward the door. Amber tries to get to them, but another negative spirit appears and holds her down to the floor. She starts to scream. Bryce is torn about what to do. He notices that the spirit is holding Amber's face to the floor in an awkward position. When Bryce turns back around, the door is starting to open slowly. He appears scared and then notices Omani in deep thought. The door keeps opening against the demon's wish that is on the other side, making it very angry. The red-glowing demon keeps trying to fight the glow that is protecting them and is slowly starting to get through. This makes it emit an evil laugh while working even harder and more aggressively to try to get through the glow.

"Hurry!!" Bryce screams.

Finally, the door opens. On the other side is something nobody is prepared for. There in the center of the bathroom is a swirling wind motion like a hurricane. In the center are many trapped souls, screaming and trying to find a way out and pushing on the sides of the hurricane. When they do, tortures begin, making them scream even more. Somehow these trapped souls are able to see Bryce and Omani and try to reach out their hands for help. But one of the demons won't have it and strikes at them, making it impossible for them to see through the intense haze. Bryce and Omani look at each other with tears rolling down their faces. They hold each others' hands while bowing their heads in sorrow. Then they hear a strange noise, causing Bryce to look up.

"Hey! There it is—the pentagram. It's behind all of that, and it's the driving force. Look!!" he says, shaking Omani's hand to get her to look up.

She looks up and catches a glimpse before the haze covers it.

"How are we supposed to get over there?" she asks.

"I have an idea. Come on," he says.

"The glow around you is fading," Omani says, very worried.

"We don't have much time. Come on!!" he says.

They go back out of the bathroom and see Amber trying to get over to them.

"Stay there!! Get those booze bottles from behind you!" Bryce says.

Amber looks and sees some half-filled bottles on the floor behind the bar area. She holds onto the bar with one hand and reaches for the bottles with the other, placing them between her legs to hold onto them. Bryce and Omani come toward her slowly.

"What are you going to do?" Omani asks.

"Create a diversion," he says, reaching over the bar to a side pocket and grabbing a lighter. There are a few towels stuck in a cabinet hanging out a little ways over the side. He reaches over and grabs them, takes the tops off the bottles, and stuffs the towels in the small openings.

"Okay, let's make a circle for just a second," he says.

They hover over the bottles while he flicks the lighter. The first couple of times the whirlwind catches it and puts it out. The demons notice that something is going on and start to come closer, making Amber very nervous. The red-glowing demon is so angry that it is pushing the other demons out of the way, rushing to get over there. Omani grabs Amber arm and holds onto her. Finally, the lighter comes up and he lights the towels. The fire begins as a flicker but quickly bursts into large peaking flames. He places one bottle on the floor where they are approaching and another by where the demons hover the most. Then he quickly dashes off for the bathroom and places one inside the doorway. The smoke causes the fire alarm to go off and the sprinkler system to kick in. The water is spraying so heavily that the spirits can't locate the trio. They hold onto each other's hands and head to the bathroom and close the door. Amber grabs the rods, Omani throws the special dust, and Bryce approaches the pentagram. The portal appears, and the rods become erect. The pentagram begins to emanate a strange glow like it's on fire.

"There's another demon trying to come through. Quick; open the bathroom door. Let's get out of here," Bryce screams.

Omani opens the door; there stands the angry red-glowing demon. His eyes are so enraged that they are blinding and mesmerizing at the same time. Omani can't take her eyes off of it, and the demon draws her in. As it gets real close to her it starts to thin out. Amber turns her head and knows her sister is in trouble. The demon is heading for her sister's nose to be inhaled.

"*Omani! No!! Bryce!*" Amber yells.

He turns around, noticing what's happening, and breaks away from the pentagram. The next demon comes through more terrifying than the previous ones. Bryce comes up to Omani and grabs her arm to snap her out of it. The demon screeches loudly and retreats. Bryce takes her by the hand and turns around to head back to the pentagram only to be met by the next demon. It pushes Bryce away against the wall, knocking him out.

"Close your eyes, Omani!" Amber says to her sister telepathically.

Omani closes her eyes, trying to fight another demon, that is staring directly in her face trying to thin out. Amber notices that the attention is solely on her sister and heads toward the pentagram. She sees the lighter on the floor next to the sink, and she picks it up and breaks it open. Then she splashes it on the drawing. The fire invigorates. All the demons quickly turn their attention to Amber and what she is doing and storm in her direction. She splashes the pentagram again and then puts down the empty lighter and grabs the rods while throwing the powder. Omani opens her eyes and looks over at her sister. The demons are closing in on her. She runs to her sister's side and holds her hands to guide the rods. They become erect. The demons form a line going toward the portal. They fight it, trying to find a way to stay. But the power is too strong. It pulls them in and closes after the last one goes through it. The whirlwind stops, and the place quickly lightens up. The hurricane formed around the trapped souls stops. The sisters stand there in shock. Bryce wakes up, massaging his head from the impact. Omani approaches the trapped souls. Amber watches her, not knowing what's going on but sensing many presences. She curiously watches her sister.

"You're free now. Go to where you need to be, and be safe," Omani says.

The trapped souls sway up to the ceiling and disappear. Bryce stands up and approaches Omani. She turns around and notices the guy who was murdered standing there. He looks at her with great thanks. She smiles at him, and he disappears. Then they hear voices in the vicinity. Three men come into the bathroom. Two are dressed in firemen's attire with axes in their hands. The other is one of the owners all worked up and freaking out about what's happening. The firefighters just continue doing their job and calling for someone to take the owner away.

"Are you all right?" a firefighter asks.

"We're fine; thanks," Amber replies.

"Hey, do you know why no one has taken this pentagram down?" Omani asks.

"We tried several times, but it always comes back. We just figured someone keep drawing it back up there again," the owner states.

"Well, they're not anything to play with, and I think you may want to have this place blessed, and soon. Come on," Omani says.

"By the way, nice sprinkler system," Bryce says as he walks past the three guys. The trio is almost to the door when they stop and take a deep breath.

"Are you okay?" Amber asks her sister.

"Yeah. I don't know what happened. It's like it had a hold on me or something. That was a different kind of power, and it was strong. Thanks for helping me. Bryce, are you okay?" Omani asks.

She touches his head softly, feeling it. He becomes squeamish and groans when she gets to the tender spot.

"I've got some tender love for that," she says, kissing him.

"I think it's time to get you two love birds home," Amber says.

"Is it just me or are these things getting stronger?" Bryce asks, still massaging his head.

"They know that we're here. They aren't going to stop until they have Vuex. Plus, hate to break it to you, but that wasn't even the big one yet that Grandma talked about," Omani replies.

"Makes me look forward to tomorrow. *Hah!!* So what was that about tender love?" Bryce says.

"Come on," Omani says.

The trio walk out of the bar, looking beat up but not beaten. They walk across the street and head toward their car as the city lights shine bright against the dark sky.

CHAPTER 15

At mid-morning the clock is ticking with every second sounding more intense than the previous one; today is the big day for the band. Everything seems to be going well. Outside, the sun is shining and the birds are singing. But inside, in the kitchen, stands a nervous Omani, opening cabinets and looking for something. Each time she grabs for something she appears to have butterfingers. Everything slips right through her hands either to the counter or the floor. The fourth time this happens, she sighs, slapping her right hand to her thigh and using her left hand to hold back her hair. She tries one more time and reaches for the coffee can on the top shelf of the cupboard. This time three things fall.

"That's it!!" she says, kicking the items on the floor.

Bryce is standing by the door, quietly observing the whole scenario. He can't help but chuckle.

"What are you laughing at?" she says.

"You're so cute when you get angry. What's the matter, anyway?" he asks, coming the rest of the way into the kitchen.

"I don't know. Nerves I guess," she says, putting her head down to the floor.

Bryce can tell that Omani is about to cry. He quickly and quietly goes to her side and lifts her chin with one hand, guiding her eyes to meet his with no words spoken. She gazes into his eyes, getting lost.

"It's going to be okay. I want you to think positive. Today I'll handle the small stuff. I want you to get ready for tonight, okay? And we won't do any guardian stuff today. The band is our bread and butter. You sit down and let me get the coffee," he says, guiding her to a chair.

"I can't help but think about last time," she says.

"This time will be different," Bryce says with utmost confidence.

"What's going on?" Amber asks.

"Jitters," Bryce replies.

"Oh yeah. Me too. Kyle, can I call you later?" she says with the phone up to the ear.

Amber hangs up the phone and pulls up a chair next to her sister. Bryce brews the coffee and serves both the ladies and himself.

"I still can't get what happened last night out of my head," Amber starts to comment.

"Yeah, I don't think people realize what they're messing with when they draw pentagrams or get out Ouija boards. They're not games. I'm just glad we had abilities to help those trapped souls," Omani replies.

"But how many more are out there just like that?" Amber asks.

"I don't know. I guess we can just hope not many," Omani says.

Omani's phone rings. Bryce runs to get it, trying to keep the ladies from getting up. He talks in code to keep them feeling at ease and ready to start the day. But Omani knows that something is up. She becomes quiet and listens to his whispering, trying to make out the conversation. She can only catch a few words, so she gets up with the cup of coffee in her hands and goes on to the entryway of the kitchen to get a better sense of the conversation. After a few seconds she realizes that it's the band. There's a problem, and Bryce is keeping it secret. She marches right up to him and stares at him, wanting an answer. He just smiles and turns away. She sighs and gets back up into his face. Bryce hangs up.

"How's the coffee?" he asks.

"Don't change the subject on me. What's going on? That was Trent, wasn't it?" Omani states.

Bryce knows he can't pull one over on her, so he hangs his head a little.

"Yes. But everything is okay. He just had trouble finding a piece of equipment," Bryce replies.

"Equipment, my ass! Trent doesn't call for something like that. What's going on?" she says again but more firmly and reaches for the phone and dials a number. Bryce grabs it out of her hands while Amber watches with big eyes.

"I told you I'm handling the small stuff. You just focus on tonight," he says.

"Bryce!!" she begins to say, but she's interrupted.

"No woman of mine is going to be stressed out on an important day. I've got it, and I mean it," he explains, ready to defend his actions.

She turns and starts to stomp away angrily. He grabs her by the arm and quickly turns her back around. Just as she is facing him, he pulls her close and kisses her passionately. Amber smiles and tiptoes back into the kitchen. Omani pulls away and slaps Bryce, looking at him with intense anger. But those angered eyes quickly turn to affectionate looks as she finds herself kissing him again but even more passionately. After a few minutes of intense kissing he whispers in her ear that everything is going to be fine.

Later that day everyone is a bundle of nerves. Bryce is at the venue where the performance is going to occur, sitting down and playing his acoustic guitar as a calming mechanism. The only other person there is the bar owner, who is preparing for the night while smoking a cigarette. Bryce keeps playing the same song over and over again, staring into space in deep thought. David and Gabe get out of the car having a major discussion.

"But seriously, what are you going to do if this doesn't happen?" Trent asks, grabbing equipment out of the trunk. Gabe stops what he's doing and gives Trent a long nasty glare.

"You know, I've had just about enough of this. You're already talking like we're doomed. Think positive, man. For crying out loud, the agents sought us out after listening to the CD we submitted, and don't forget it. Oh, and if it doesn't happen then I'll cross that road when I get to it. But the one comment I haven't heard from you is what you are going to do if we get the deal. Start thinking that way, and maybe people will respond to you better," Gabe replies.

He leans over and grabs his last-minute items and walks off with his girlfriend, not waiting for Mr. Downer. Trent just stands there realizing the strength of Gabe's statement. He picks up his outfit bag and begins walking to the building. Upon entering, Gabe hears the acoustic guitar. He puts his stuff down to see what's going on.

"Hey, you're here early," Gabe says.

"Yeah. Thought I would warm up for tonight," Bryce replies.

"So where are Omani and Amber?" Gabe asks.

"Getting ready. They'll be here," Bryce replies somberly, not looking at him.

Meanwhile, across town Omani is sitting in a beautician's chair with wet hair. A man stands behind her with a pair of scissors. On the table in front of her are some magazines with different haircuts and styles.

"I like this one," Omani says.

The beautician frowns after looking at the picture and then at her.

"I'm going to be honest with you; with that face that hairdo won't work. Now, is there a special occasion or something?" he asks.

"Yes, I'm in a band, and we're singing in front of agents tonight to try to get a contract," she replies.

He takes his hand and gently sweeps his fingers through her hair, thinking and staring into the mirror at her face. He sighs a few times as he continues stroking the hair.

"How open are you to a new look?" he asks.

She turns around and looks at him in the eyes. She remembers what Bryce said, and it starts to echo in her mind again.

"Very," she says with a serious face.

He swings the chair away from the mirror and toward him.

"Then I know exactly what we're going to do, and you can't peek until we're done. And you know what? I had a cancellation after you, so I would be happy to do your makeup too," he replies.

Omani smiles.

Amber is in another salon doing the same thing. The lady beautician is looking over pictures with her on a sofa. Amber pinches a corner of the paper back on a page when she finds something that may be of interest. After flipping through several more pages and almost reaching the end of the book, Amber begins to turn to the next page. The beautician slams her hand down on the current page to quickly stop Amber.

"There! I think with a little tweaking that style is perfect for you," the lady says.

Amber looks at her, thrown by it all.

"Are you sure?" she replies.

"Yep. I can see the end product already. Come on. It's time to glam you up," she says, getting up walking with the book in her hand.

There's a forty-five minute before it's time for the band to perform. Gabe and Bryce are doing sound checks again for the third time. Bryce is setting the stage for moving around and trying different movements and seeing where he lands. He looks to see where the agents are going to be placed to view the band and maneuvers things a little further. He places himself in different areas of the stage based on where everyone else will be standing. Bryce finally gets it right and smiles. Gabe can tell, though, that Bryce is a little different than his usual self.

"Trent, you've got it?" Gabe asks.

"Yeah. Just about done," Trent responds.

"Okay, I'm going to get ready," Gabe says and then kisses his girlfriend.

Gabe notices Bryce heading to the back and quickly tries to catch up to him. Bryce reaches for his duffel bag and sets it on a table and opens it. There's a picture of his previous band on top. Gabe comes up slowly and quietly behind him.

"Hey, you ready?" Gabe asks.

Bryce quickly puts the picture down and turns around.

"Yeah. I can't wait for the opportunity," he replies.

Gabe sees the picture.

"I heard," Gabe says, pointing to the picture.

Bryce gives a somber look while glancing at the picture again. He puts his hands in his pockets, trying not to get choked up.

"Yeah. Tonight's the first time I've performed in front of an audience since that tragedy. This night means more to me than a contract. Music was our world. This tattoo represents that, and I wear it proudly. I need to prove that their deaths and what we stood for weren't in vain," Bryce says, showing his tattoo with the band name and a heart with dripping blood. Then he continues getting things out of his duffel bag. Gabe looks at him with the utmost respect and admiration. Something like a light bulb goes on, and then Trent comes around the corner.

"Tonight I plan on giving hundred and fifty percent. I think you should too," Gabe says to Trent in a serious and determined voice.

"Who says I won't?" Trent replies with a cocky attitude.

"You know what I mean," Gabe replies, glaring at Trent.

He hangs his head slightly and nods, knowing that his friend isn't going to back down.

Fifteen minutes before starting time for the band the guys sit very anxiously in the back of the club. Gabe's legs are twitching, and Trent is biting the sides of his fingers and sitting forward in his chair. Bryce is kicked back in the chair, looking relaxed and almost at peace with himself. All three of them look fantastic. But Bryce stands out the most with his suave hairstyle, a hot rocking shirt, sexy white jeans, and thin snake print trench coat with with cut out diamond shapes in the arms. The coat complements his tattoos, making people want to look at them. Trent has on a rocking shirt, but it's just not as sharp. His tattoo isn't as striking but is still noticeable. Gabe is wearing dark jeans and a shirt that screams to the girls "come and get me." His hair is slicked back like a gangster, giving him the bad-boy look. Trent repositions himself in the chair and looks around the room.

"So where are Omani and Amber? They should have been here at least fifteen minutes ago," Trent says.

"Relax. They'll be here," Bryce replies.

Just then, the manager comes back.

"You guys ready? The agents have just been seated. We've got a full house and then some. I'm thinking of getting you out there a few minutes early. I'm going to do the introductions in about five to ten minutes," he says and bolts back out, not noticing that the ladies aren't there.

Gabe and Trent get up and start pacing the floor like a father waiting for his first baby to be born. Bryce just watches them, staying cool. The guys don't speak to each other since they are in deep thought. The clock on the wall ticks louder with each second. They didn't notice it before, but now every second sounds like a sonic boom. About ten minutes later the manager comes back, all excited.

"Ready?" he says.

"Uhh … uhh … where are the ladies?" Trent says again.

Just then, they hear the back entrance door open. Trent is standing there with his hands on his hips ready to lay into them about their tardiness. But then around the corner come two almost unrecognizable women. Trent's angered diminishes and turns to shock, and his hands go down to his sides. Bryce is sitting relaxed, but as soon as he gets a small glimpse at Omani he sits straight up. He couldn't take his eyes off of her. Gabe looks at both ladies, speechless. As they come toward the guys it's like they're walking in slow motion. Bryce slowly rises from his chair. Omani is dressed in a red and black jumpsuit with a jagged cut style with black python shoes that wrap around the leg. Her jumpsuit has a very sexy open back with a tattoo of the four winds symbol showing. Her hair is cut shorter, with a beautiful look of old Hollywood glamour to it. On the outside of her hair gold strings glitter in the light, catching everyone's attention. They don't overshadow her hair but instead blend in quite nicely. Her face and new hairstyle mesmerize people as they stare at her. Amber is wearing a coral low-cut cold shoulder top with lace sleeves. She has on brown leather pants that have guitar cut out designs on each thigh with strings that glow. The whole outfit screams with rocking style. Her hair is cut as well, with flowing curls. Both their faces are glowing in a way no one had ever seen before.

"Sorry we're late. It took longer than expected to get ready," Omani replies.

Trent just looks at her, speechless and not knowing what to do or say. Bryce walks slowly up to Omani with his eyes still enlarged.

"*Wow!!*" he says, looking her up and down.

"It was your idea, remember? Speaking of ideas, I love the look," she says, flirtatiously touching him.

"Thanks, baby. I'm glad you listened. You're going to knock their socks off!! ," he states.

"Amber I never thought ... if Kyle could only see you," Gabe remarks.

Before they can further discuss the ladies' looks, they can hear the manager talking on the microphone. Suddenly the sexy and confident Omani turns into a bundle of nerves.

"Is everything set up? What about the sound checks? The stage preparation?" Omani keeps thinking of more stuff.

Bryce grabs her hands and holds them close to her chest as he moves close to her heart.

"It's all been taken care of. I just want you glow tonight," Bryce says, calming her down. He does a few deep breaths with her. While he is doing that Gabe and Trent look Amber up and down. Trent even lifts his eyebrows a few times at her. She is not fascinated by his flirtatious behavior. Instead she smiles and then starts walking toward the stage door. Bryce takes Omani's hand and guides her to where Amber is standing. The manager is still talking.

"Okay, I know it's a little late, but remember that this is all for one and one for all. We can do this. Even if you mess up keep going. This is our night," Omani says.

"We will get this contract!" Amber says, following her.

Just then the manager announces the band's name and the light is turned toward the back door. It's their cue, and they all head out to the stage listening to the clapping and the roar of the crowd . All of their hearts are beating fast. The night is about to begin.

CHAPTER 16

THE BAND IS ON stage with lights beaming down on them. It seems surreal, so they are all taking in the moment to remember it. Finally, the clapping subsides and the band begins to play in harmony. Omani can't help but look over to where the agents are sitting and looking toward the stage. Her hands tremble slightly, but she quickly pulls it together. Amber looks over there for a second and then quickly focuses on the music. All the guys are just into the music and are not paying attention to who is out there. Omani turns her head away from the microphone for a second to cough and clear the throat. Then she begins to sing. Her voice sounds angelic and effortless. Amber chimes in, making the music that much more intriguing. When the first song is done the audience can't help but clap. Omani smiles and looks over to the agents. They aren't clapping. In fact, one has his arms crossed. She swallows and looks back at the band and smiles, trying to calm herself. They start the next song and Bryce strikes his electric guitar, turning all the women in the audience on. Some stand up, while others race to the stage. One person throws a pair of underwear onto the stage. Omani and Amber look at each other, almost laughing, but go on. As they perform song after song everything is on target. They make one mistake, but the band plays through it quite well. When they finish one song a stool is placed behind Omani. Bryce taps her shoulder. She sits down and looks at the audience lovingly.

"I want to thank everyone for coming out tonight. You know that we write songs for different reasons. There are a lot of things that inspire us, like love, family, or even a special place. But there's one area of inspiration that we especially want to acknowledge, and that is you. To thank you, we came up with a couple of special songs to let you know how much our hearts have been touched. The first one is a little slow, and then the next one gives each band member a chance to show what they've got as a tribute to you. Thanks again, and enjoy," Omani says, getting up from the stool with the crowd roaring with excitement.

Gabe starts to play a slow harmony on the keyboard, Bryce softly plays his acoustic guitar, and Trent taps the drums to give a nice mellow sound. Omani and Amber come together, hugging each other with one arm while facing the audience, and start singing. Omani can't help but notice a black squiggly figure dash across the top of the audience up to the ceiling. She blocks it out and continues. But then another comes swooping from another direction. She looks at Amber, concerned and trying to let her know that something is wrong. Amber continues to sing, not noticing. When the song comes to an end, Omani breathes a deep sigh. She keeps saying to herself under her breath that they only have three songs left. However, the next three songs are the ones they have practiced the most in order to impress the agents and get the contract. They are their ending punch. Omani closes her eyes, hoping they can complete the songs. As they start the first song the lights begin to flicker. Omani quickly looks at Bryce, and he gives her a nod to keep going. She looks over and sees that all the agents are still there. It's different from last time. Two of them seemed engrossed in the music. This makes her very happy and nervous at the same time, as the flickering action intensifies. Bryce is playing his guitar, making the men wish they can play like him; all the women have love-glazed eyes. He strikes a chord that signifies to Omani to begin singing. Just as she starts the lights go out and the whole place is pitch black. Not even the emergency lights come on. The crowd starts to scream. Omani and the band stop performing at the same time because it's too hard to perform over the screaming. Omani hangs her head with tears rolling down her cheeks. They hear people trying to push through the entryway to get out. Nobody can tell if the agents are still there since it's so dark, although Amber does try to look. This event is just too much for Omani. They can hear footsteps stomping off stage.

"Omani?" Amber asks, holding out her arms and trying to feel her way to where her sister is standing. She can't feel anything but air.

"Omani??!! Are you there?" Amber asks again but louder and in a more desperate plea. She gets no response. Somebody touches her back, and Amber turns around to grab the hand.

"Omani, is that you?" she asks.

"No, it's Bryce," he replies.

"I can't find her," Amber replies, panicking.

"Stay right here. I'll be right back," he says.

The lights are still off in the building, and people are screaming and scrambling to get out. Gabe, Trent, and Amber stand together in a huddle. Bryce feels his way off stage and heads to the back hallway. He bangs into the door and the walls a few times, trying to find his way out. He finally pushes a door open and gets outside. The street lamps are out in the immediate area and people are running everywhere. The moon is shining down, providing just enough light to see around him. He sees in the not-too-far distance somebody sitting on what appears to be a log with their head down. He quickly goes over there and taps the person on the shoulders, hearing sobbing as the person lifts her face.

"Leave me alone!!" Omani says.

"Omani, listen to me!" Bryce says, trying to calm her by touching and caressing her arm. She jerks her arm away and gets up, taking a few steps away from him with tears flowing down her face.

"No!! You don't understand!!!!! I have worked my whole life for this, and for what? To watch it go up in smoke!! I can't take this anymore. What they hell am I supposed to do now? My hopes and dreams are gone, all because of these ... these ... nasty fucking entities! I'm never going to be free of them, am I? This was supposed to be our night!! *Our night!!* Now it's *gone forever!!!*" Omani screams, running up to a nearby pole and hitting it, making her hand start to bleed. Bryce quickly runs up to her as she feels that all hope is gone and loses control. He grabs her hands; she fights to get them free. But the harder she pulls, the more he holds on. Her crying is out of control.

"Omani, listen to me," he says in a calming voice.

"No. No more," she says as her hands break free. She starts running, and he takes off after her down the street. There's a car coming, and the driver isn't watching where he's going. The car is heading straight for Omani, who is so upset that she is not aware of her surroundings.

"Omani. Look out!!" Bryce screams while continuing to run after her.

She's crying loudly, not listening. Somehow, Bryce gets a surge of energy that makes him run faster. The car is quickly approaching Omani. As Bryce gets close to her he hears the sound of squealing tires.

Omani stops at the sound and quickly turns around and screams, seeing blinding headlights directly in front of her. Suddenly she is pushed to the ground and the tires pass by just a few inches from her arm. The driver stops and gets out, running to the back of the vehicle. He sees a man on top of a woman.

"Are you all right?" he asks.

"We're fine," Bryce says.

The man gets back into this car and scurries away. Bryce gets up just enough to see Omani's face. She begins to speak, but he places his hand on her mouth to quiet her.

"I listened to what you had to say. I don't blame you for being upset. But this is not the end of the world. The night isn't over yet. We need to get back in there and play. I'm not going to let this night go up in smoke, and neither should you. We can fight this together," he says.

She moves his hand, wiping her tears away, and sniffles a few times to clear her nose.

"How are we going to play with no electricity?" she asks.

"You remember when you told me that this happened before?" he states.

"Yeah," she replies.

"Well, let's just say I came prepared," he says.

He gets off of her and stands up, holding out his hand to help her up. She reaches out to him as he pulls her up close to him.

"Do you think the agents are still there?" she asks.

"Only one way to find out. I want you to sing a solo from your heart, okay?" he says.

"What?" she replies.

"Trust me. Come on," he says, holding her hand and guiding her back to the club.

As they approach the building they see that the lights are still out. Bryce goes up to the back door and opens it.

"Hold onto my shirt," he says.

They enter the building and feel their way back to the stage. The screaming has subsided. Their footsteps resound as they get back on the stage.

"Omani?" Amber asks.

"Yeah. I'm okay," she replies, hugging her sister.

They hear the sound of a lighter being struck. Bryce is lighting candles one by one around the stage. It looks beautiful when he finishes. Omani turns and looks at him with great adoration. He just smiles and continues on. Then she looks out to the audience and notices that there are still people seated. Omani slowly starts to look over to where the agents were sitting, but she can't bring herself to actually look at the seats. Can she handle it if they aren't there? She can feel her heart sink into her chest as she tries to look again, but she still can't look. Bryce hands her the microphone, and she clips it back on, just in case. She swings her pretty hair back and accidentally catches a glimpse of the area where the agents were seated. Her jaw drops when she sees two of them still seated there. She looks at everyone in the band with amazement, like it's a miracle. Bryce takes a seat and places the acoustic guitar on his lap. He begins to stroke it. Omani is so touched that she doesn't know what to think or say. She feels a sensation of great gratitude coming over her, and she starts to sing from her heart. The song hasn't ever been done before tonight. Tears flow from her face naturally as she sings. The agents get up and actually try to get closer to the stage. Absorbed in the song, Omani isn't even paying attention. Amber, Gabe, and Trent have their arms around each other and are softly humming in the background. When the song was done there isn't a dry eye in the room. Even the agents have to wipe their eyes. Omani goes over to Bryce and holds out her hand. He doesn't know what to think, so he just stands up quietly. The room is silent.

"I love you," she whispers softly, but everyone can hear it.

She gently and passionately kisses him. The audience that remains claps and gives a standing ovation. Omani turns around in shock and wipes her eyes again, astonished and embarrassed. The rest of the band rushes to her side and does a group hug. The agents don't wait for them to come down off the stage. Instead they begin to climb up, but the manager approaches and stops them.

"Now that the performance is over I have to have everyone exit the building. Fire code safety," he says.

The agents look at each other in agreement and then look at the band and smile and turn and walk away. They're almost to the door when Omani realizes what's happening.

"Wait! Did we get the contract?" she says, but it's too late; the front door is closed.

She is very disheartened. Bryce looks at her.

"They have your number. I think they were impressed," he says.

"We'd better get going," Gabe says.

"Hey, what's with the strange-looking cloud?" Trent says.

Amber, Omani, and Bryce are talking to each other when Trent's question hits them. They suddenly stop talking and look around.

"Trent, get away from there!" Amber shouts.

"What? I'm just picking up the drumstick that fell to the ground," he replies.

Suddenly the squiggly figures appear again as the cloud takes a more intense shape. Trent is still leaning over and drops the drumstick again. As he kneels down with one foot sticking out slightly, the squiggly things start to move in. The trio starts to walk across the stage to where Trent is kneeling. Lightning streaks appear as they walk. Gabe notices and backs away, not knowing what to think.

"Trent, get up," Amber says.

"Got it," he says as he begins to get up.

But then a huge arm comes out of the mysterious cloud and grabs his foot as it sticks out. Trent nudges it to get it free. He tries a couple of times but then realizes that it's stuck to something. He turns to look and sees a huge arm holding onto his foot. He looks up in the cloud and sees evil-looking face staring at him. He starts to scream. The trio runs to his side, but the thing has other ideas. It's very strong and pulls Trent into the mysterious cloud and quickly disappears. Gabe's mouth is hanging open in fright.

"Where's Trent? What happened to Trent? What was that?" Gabe says, horrified.

"That wasn't a portal. What was that?" Amber asks.

"I don't know, but whatever it was this isn't good. I think our nightmare has just begun," Omani replies.

They turn to look at Gabe, who is shaking in his shoes and staring at the spot where Trent disappeared.

They rush over to him.

"Gabe, we'll take care of it," Amber says.

"Did you see that?" Gabe says.

"He's in shock. Let's sit him down. Bryce, get him some water," Omani says.

Amber and Omani calmly sit Gabe down. He just stares into space, bewildered.

"It's like the devil himself came and took him away," Gabe says.

"Gabe, look at me," Omani says, touching his face softly and guiding his eyes to hers. It takes him a few seconds for him to focus. In a daze, he looks into her eyes.

"Do you believe in heaven and hell?" Omani asks.

"Yeah," he responds.

"Well, there's a bit of a war going on right now, and unfortunately Trent just got placed in the middle of it. We're going to go get him. I want you to stay somewhere safe, so we're going to take you to a hospital to sit in the emergency room with your girlfriend. We'll come back for you, okay? Gabe, nod if you understand," Omani says.

He nods, but it's obvious that he's not all there. Amber gives him a sip of water. He almost forgets how to swallow and starts coughing. He takes another sip. Omani looks over to Bryce.

"We don't have much time. We've got to go to Zadku's Point and now!" she says.

"Let's take him to the car. Amber, Omani, hold onto my shirt with one hand and hold onto Gabe with the other," Bryce says.

It takes some time, but they get to the car.

"Wow, he's really in shock," Amber says.

"Wouldn't you be?" Omani replies.

Bryce drives off in a hurry to the hospital, running a few lights to get there as fast as possible. He pulls up in front of the emergency room doors and they quickly escort Gabe out of the car and into a seat. The emergency room is full, and nobody even notices them.

"Maybe we should take him with us," Amber says.

"No, I don't think he'll be able to handle it. He'll be safe here. Gabe, Cheryl, we'll be back. Stay here, okay?" Omani says.

"Okay," Cheryl says.

"Trust me; I'm staying in the light," he replies.

The trio hugs him, and then they take off to the car.

"Do you have the map? I have a feeling we're in for something that we haven't seen before, but we've got to get Trent," Omani says.

Bryce nods his head. The car speeds off toward a bank of ominous clouds with strange lightning streaks that hang in the mist.

CHAPTER 17

WHEN THE TRIO HAS been on the road for over five hours there's the hint of daylight across the sky in the distance. They are surrounded by desert, with no signs of civilization. Both the ladies are asleep, and Bryce is very sleepy but tries to stay awake. He slams his eyes open whenever his head bobs forward and turns on the air conditioner and rolls down the window as a staying-awake mechanism. Eventually, the cold air begins to fill the car, causing Omani to start to wake up. As she begins to open her eyes, the car comes to a stop.

"Where are we?" she asks.

"We're here," he replies.

Omani looks around and notices some hills along with mountains but overall just sees desert. She looks at him with concern as though he has just flipped his lid. Bryce just opens the car door, which startles Amber awake. She looks around and then looks at her sister, wondering what is happening.

"Come on," he says.

They get out the car slowly and hesitantly. Bryce opens the trunk and grabs two duffel bags and hands one to Amber and places the other shoulder. They start walking to somewhere unknown.

"*Wait!* This way," Omani says.

"How do you know?" Bryce asks.

"I don't know there's just something pulling me to go this way," she replies.

He shrugs his shoulders, and they start to walk in that direction. The day starts out pretty cool, but as soon as the sun starts to shine the heat begins. After walking for about two hours, they stop and look around. The car is nowhere in sight anymore. In fact, there isn't even a road near where they are standing. There's nothing but desert everywhere. There's some rough terrain ahead that looks to be fatal if not handled correctly, so they take drinks of water, trying to remain calm. After a few more minutes they start walking again. As they begin to traverse the rough terrain they see dead animal bones lying around, so the trio watches their steps. Amber looks around feeling concerned and lost, wondering how much further they need to go. Bryce just takes it in stride and keeps going. After two more hours they stop again for a water break and wiping away perspiration. This time Omani wanders a few feet away from the other two. She looks around, getting a strange sensation. After Bryce takes a few sips of water from his bottle, he notices her looking around.

"How much longer? It's really getting hot out here," Amber says.

Omani continues looking around, almost as though she didn't hear her sister.

"What's going on?" Bryce asks.

"Do you have Grandma's glasses?" she asks.

"Huh? You're supposed to be able to see spirits without them," Amber replies.

"I know. Do you have them?" she says, looking away while requesting them.

Amber frowns and kneels down; she and Bryce look through the duffel bags.

"Here they are," he says, handing them to Omani.

She steps further away from them, staring into the desert.

"What's going on?" Amber asks confused. She even tries to reach her sister telepathically and gets no response.

"I don't know," Bryce replies, watching Omani.

She gets to a certain point and stops. Omani kneels down and places the glasses on the ground. Amber and Bryce look at each other, puzzled, while wiping the sweat away from their brows. They see her wandering off a little farther and decide to go catch up. Out in the desert a person never knows what may be lurking. Omani seems to be trying to place the glasses strategically in the dirt.

"What are you doing?" Amber asks.

"Those glasses aren't just for seeing spirits," Omani replies.

"I know. But what's going on?" Bryce asks.

Omani steps back, and the other two watch her, wondering what's going on. As the glaring sun hits the sunglasses, a beam of light shoots off of them and toward the open desert. Suddenly the desolate desert turns into a picture, with green grass and a few trees and a stream. Off in the distance is a low mountain with a strange-looking temple pyramid-type building on top of it. The temple is made of stone with various pieces of beautiful metal decorating it. It's covered with strange markings in a lost language now unknown to man.

"Do you see anything?" Amber asks.

"Yeah," Bryce replies, bewildered.

"That's where we're going. Toward the stone temple," Omani says, pointing while she picks up the glasses.

The temple that appeared with the glasses is now gone, but the small mountain is still there.

"Where's the temple?" Amber asks.

"Well, if you look closely, that other small mountain wasn't there. So it must be hidden behind it. Come on," Omani replies.

They all forget about the desert heat and take off for the lost temple. As they travel up through a small path to get around the first small mountain small dark clouds begin to form.

"Good, looks like some rain relief," Amber says.

Bryce looks up, noticing the clouds.

"Those aren't rain clouds. Keep moving," he says.

As they get past the first mountain, there's a small rope bridge traversing a huge drop below and connecting on the other side to where they need to be. Amber sees the flimsy rope bridge and stops; Omani is about to take the first step.

"We have to cross *that?*" Amber says.

"Either that or we can roll down the big hill, get a few bruises, and then climb up to the other side if we're lucky," Bryce says sarcastically.

Omani lifts a foot to place it on the bridge.

"*Stop!*" Amber yells, running up to her sister. "We don't know how sturdy that is."

Bryce shakes it to see what happens. It makes a little noise, but nothing snaps.

"One at a time," Bryce says.

"I can't cross that," Amber says.

"You have to. I'll go first," Omani says.

Amber stands there shaking and watching her sister begin to cross. The rope makes no sound when Omani has one foot on it, but when she places both feet on it they can hear tension noises. Amber takes both of her hands and covers her face, unable to watch.

"No fast moves," Bryce says calmly.

Omani slowly crosses as the tension noises become more intense. Just as the noises start to become scary, almost like a snapping sound, she successfully makes it to the other side, screaming with excitement as though she has just won a medal. Amber opens her eyes and looks to see that her sister is okay.

"You're next," Bryce says.

Amber bites her nails in fear. Her trembling legs move slowly to the rope bridge. She backs away in intense fear. Bryce looks up, noticing the clouds, and goes over to Amber, taking her hand. He makes her concentrate on him and then tries to instill a feeling of endurance and courage in her. Omani just watches from the distance. Suddenly Amber goes over to the rope and slowly starts to walk on it. Again, it isn't until her second foot is on the rope that the tension noises begin. The duffel bag hangs off her back so that her hands are free. As she steps across the bridge the tension noises seem to intensify more than when Omani crossed. As Amber takes the next step they hear a snapping noise.

"*What was that?*" Amber says, panicking.

"Keep going; just no sudden movements," Bryce yells as Amber makes it to the halfway point.

She takes another step and hears another snap. The rope drops a little, and Amber screams, holding onto the side of the rope, afraid to go any further.

"Keep going!!" Bryce yells.

"*I can't!!*" Amber yells, terrified.

Just then she looks down and sees that it's at least a hundred feet down. She begins to shake uncontrollably. Omani is horrified as she watches her sister.

"Come on Amber," Omani says.

"*I can't!! I'm going to die!! I know it!!*" she cries.

Bryce flips the duffel bag onto his back and heads to the bridge.

"What are you doing?" Omani says.

"I'm going to help Amber," he says.

"But it won't hold both of you," Omani says.

"Got a better idea?" he asks.

Amber has tears running down her face, thinking this is the end. Bryce takes a step onto the bridge and hears the tension noise immediately start. Omani gasps, watching. With each step her heart skips a beat. Bryce places his other foot on the bridge; it starts to swing a little. The tension noises are loud and scary. He strategically and slowly places his feet to help reduce the tension so it can hold both of them. Amber's tears are coming faster as her hands are white from holding on so tight. Bryce approaches her, holding out his hand.

"Take my hand," he says.

"*I can't!*" she screams.

"*Yes, you can!* This bridge isn't going to hold much longer. Amber, you've got to get a grip. Don't look down, and take my hand," Bryce says calmly.

It takes her a few seconds to work up the courage to do as he says, and she begins to reach out her hand to his. Her hand is trembling so hard like that of a hummingbird's wings. As she clutches her hand into his, Amber takes a deep sigh of relief. Suddenly they hear another loud snapping noise, and she begins to pull away. Bryce grabs her hand and pulls her up. He places one hand around her waist and basically lifts her and carries her to the other side very quickly. When they have almost reached the other side they hear another loud snap. The rope jerks hard, and Bryce looks back and sees that one side is about to give way. He has no choice but to make quick movements. He lunges forward with Amber. Omani grabs her hand and pulls her to safe ground. Then the rope gives way on one side, falling, and the other side quickly follows. Omani looks up after getting Amber on the ground and doesn't see Bryce anywhere. She runs to the edge.

"*Bryce!! Bryce!!*" she screams.

They hear no reply, and there's no sign of the rope or bridge anywhere. The atmosphere is desolate and quiet. Omani just stands there in disbelief listening to the howling breeze. Then she falls to the ground, sobbing. Amber is horrified. She doesn't know what to do or say because she feels that it is her fault. Out of guilt she crawls over to her sister, trying to provide some sort of comfort.

"I'm sorry. It's my fault," Amber says.

Omani grabs her sister to hug her tightly, crying loudly. Amber is looking back to where the bridge was and hears something. She tries to hush her sister but has no luck. Then a hand appears on the edge.

"Omani, look!" Amber yells.

She turns and sees a hand starting to slide back down. They both get up quickly. Omani grabs the hand and starts pulling. Then another hand appears. Amber grabs it and pulls. Bryce's face appears. He pulls himself up the rest of the way and lies face down on the ground. He takes a few deep breaths to recover from his hard journey. Omani hugs her sister in excitement. After a few more breaths, Bryce gets up, only to be knocked down by an excited Omani. She kisses him so intensely that he can't breathe. He tries to get her off but then stops fighting it, almost like a surrender. He spreads his arms out on the ground. Amber laughs. After a few minutes, he moves his head from underneath her and sees something strange in the sky.

"Time to go," he says.

Omani looks up and sees the ominous sky. They realize that time is of the essence and take off running. As they go around the curve of another mountain they see the lost temple. It has slid down to where it cannot be easily seen. It appears to be in fantastic condition; just out of sight. They head directly for it. Just as they are to approach the entrance Bryce holds out both arms to stop the ladies.

"What's wrong?" Omani asks, noticing the concerned look on his face.

"The drawings; they're the same as on the map," he says.

"Yeah. So?" Amber says.

"I think I figured something out. This place is protected. We've got to figure these symbols out," he says.

"Well, we'd better do it quickly, because I think the battle is about to begin," Omani says.

Bryce pulls out the map and holds it up to the stone temple. Then he looks at the drawings on the temple. He notices the differences and similarities. One area shows strange symbols with a beast holding the people down. The other side shows symbols with a dog guarding a doorway.

"Well, according to this we need to avoid that side of the wall. We're to step only where you see this symbol," he says, pointing at the symbol of a flower with four different looking petals with cryptic writing.

"And if you're wrong?" Omani asks.

"Then I guess Trent is out of luck. I'll go first this time," he responds.

He gives a nervous smile but tries to give off an air of confidence. He places one foot lightly on the first flower symbol, swallows hard, and then places his other foot on the symbol. Nothing happens. He smiles and turns back to at the ladies.

"See," he says, but suddenly the ground begins to shake.

The ladies take a step back, not knowing what's going to happen. His eyes get really large, watching the floor. The ground shakes so hard that he leans forward, touching the side of the temple. He looks up, noticing that his hands are on symbols, but he's afraid to look to see which ones. He gently and slowly lifts one hand and sees nothing scary. Then he lifts the other and sees what appears to be a person screaming.

"Uh oh," he says quietly.

Parts of the temple's floor start to crumble away. He decides to try to go back, but the floor behind him gives way too. Then the wall starts to slide back, so he lets go and just stands still, watching the mysterious place unravel. The wall slides away, and a small dark tunnel appears. His once fearful feeling turns into an almost arrogant confidence as he cautiously steps forward into the tunnel.

"Next," he says, turning toward the ladies.

They leap strategically to the flower figure and into the tunnel. Amber dips into her duffel bag and pulls out a flashlight. She looks around and sees that there are large, strange bugs everywhere. Some look like giant beetles and others are oblong with long, hairy antennas on their backs. They all step into the center of the tunnel, trying to stay away from the bugs. Going around a corner they come upon a set of stairs.

"Where do these lead?" Bryce wonders.

"To the top of the temple," Omani responds.

"How do you know that?" he asks.

"I don't know. But it's like I've been here before," Omani says.

Before they go up the stairs, a dark cloud comes in from behind them down the tunnel.

"Let's go," he says.

They go up the stairs, trying to beat the dark cloud following them. Omani reaches the top first, and as the others follow with the cloud behind them. They are standing in a circular room with clear stones placed in what look to be particular locations. There is cryptic writing all over the walls. Amber shines the flashlight looking around, as they all admire the writing. Then, the cloud surrounds them and keeps them from being able to move anywhere.

"Get the stuff out," Omani says.

Amber opens up her duffel bag and pulls out the items inside. The rods just twirl around, not focusing on anything.

"What's happening?" Amber asks.

"It knows," Bryce replies.

In the cloud white eyes with orange pupils appear at spontaneous places but never twice in the same spot. Electrical strikes like lightning surround them as the trio tries to huddle together.

"The hair on my head is starting to stand up," Omani says.

Bryce pulls her in as close to him as possible. The cloud circles in closer and tighter, leaving them nowhere to go. The rods are still spinning out of control. Then, they hear a stone moving from above and a strange light enters. Suddenly, the writing on the wall begins to glow.

"Put those down," Bryce says.

Amber tries to let go but can't no matter how hard she tries. Omani reaches out and grabs them and tries to drop them but is unsuccessful. Suddenly, lightning strikes near Omani's back. She stands erect with her mouth open in shock. Bryce lets go, just staring at her with fear in his eyes. She tries to talk but can't. Then her eyes change. Bryce doesn't know what to make of it. The walls begin to glow even brighter. Bryce grabs the glasses and puts them on and looks around. His mouth drops open as he looks all around him. The writing becomes something he can understand. It states Zadku's Point and detailed information about the hierarchy of angels. Then he see two figures dressed in hooded monk outfits with the checks and balance symbols. Bryce realizes they are dominions and looks at them in awe. It's like coming to a standstill. He quickly snaps out of it and turns his head to see what is going on with Omani. That's when the rods stop and turn, pointing directly at Omani. Amber looks at her sister, not knowing what to do. She and Bryce look at each other, feeling helpless. Then the rocks that seem to be specially positioned start to glow and move.

"What's going on?" Amber asks.

"I don't know. Get the dust!!" he says.

She reaches into the bag and pulls out the canister. Opening it, she tries to throw the dust around them. But the cloud takes the dust and puts it back into the container and shuts it. Amber stands there in shock with her mouth open, not believing her eyes.

"*Whoa!*" Bryce says.

He looks at Omani and notices that her eyes are glowing; not a red color but more of a shiny glistening white. Somehow she is moved without walking to the edge of the makeshift balcony between two large stones. Bryce tries to reach out to her, but a lightning strike hits him on the hand and leaves a mark. He looks at it, massaging it from the sting.

"They're going to kill us, aren't they?" Amber asks.

"I'm not so sure. Look!" he says, pointing at the walls. The writing on the wall changes right in front of Bryce. Amber stares at it watching the glow change to a bright white. Then, Amber looks off to the distance and sees another cloud like the one at the club beginning to form. It looks totally different from the ones around them.

"What's going on?" Amber asks.

"I don't know, but it's giving us leeway to get back. Come on," he says, guiding her to the other side of the wall. The two stones Omani is standing between strike lights of different-colored rays into her, and she is lifted off the ground about two feet. Her hands hang down by her side like she has no control. Then, out from the wall come bird-size transparent angels with wings that surround Omani and begin dancing while circling her. More angels appear that are slightly larger that stand above Omani's head dumping a sparkling dust over her. In the upper corners of the room are large motionless archangels that appear ready for battle at any second. The other cloud gets close to Omani, and a huge demonic head pops out, roaring. The archangels suddenly move in for battle and approach the demon at lightning speed. The standoff is about to begin.

"What happening to her?" Amber asks still confused.

"I think we are seeing the power of Vuex come to life. Hold on. I think we're in for a bumpy ride," Bryce replies.

CHAPTER 18

Amber and Bryce are at a standstill, staring at the demonic head that has peeped out of a very dark cloud. It has malicious eyes and a deeply angry expression on its face. It looks as though it is ready to kill anything that moves, but it's focused solely on Omani. It sees how her eyes are changing and that she appears to be undergoing a metamorphosis. Her body seems to be paralyzed while this transformation is taking place, and a protective yellow cloud is surrounding her. The archangels launch arrows with flaming dust at the demon keeping it away. The evil roars again and dives out of the cloud with a very long snake-like body covered in scales and with what appears to be blistering thorns and horns. It dashes toward Omani at full force, but the arrows force it to move away. As the sky changes colors and becomes threatening, Bryce grabs Amber and gets down on the ground.

"We've got to do something," Amber whispers loudly.

"Not yet. Just stay back," Bryce says.

Amber reaches over, not taking her eyes off the nasty-looking demon. She feels her way around, trying to locate the rods that Omani dropped on the ground. She finds them and picks them up. They're still moving in a circular pattern, unable to focus on anything. Bryce places the canister in the bag; Amber grabs it, trying to open it, but can't. The demonic entity gets right into Omani's face, staring directly into her eyes, ready for battle. It uses the end of its tail to sweep across the deck, trying to knock over the strategically marked stones. One starts to wobble, and the entity starts to laugh. Then, it screams as an arrow hits it in the chest. It moves away again trying to swing at the archangels, but misses. Suddenly Omani's eyes open. They are of a different color and appearance. They look like those of a goddess ready for war. The entity backs up farther, taken aback by her appearance. Then it roars and lunges toward her. The cloud that was surrounding her is now starting to fade away. The angels around her leave.

"Where's the cloud and angels going?" Amber asks, terrified.

"I think sleeping beauty just woke up," Bryce replies.

"*Omani!*" Amber yells.

Bryce places his hands over her mouth before any more words can come out.

"That isn't the same Omani. I don't know entirely what this power of Vuex is or what it has done to her. We need to stay back," Bryce whispers.

"But we can't just let that thing attack her," Amber says, pulling his hand away and starting to stand up.

The demonic entity sees Amber and backs up and then suddenly lunges in her direction. She starts to scream, and Omani turns around. Amber becomes speechless with her mouth open when she sees her sister's glowing eyes. The demonic entity reaches for Amber, but Bryce grabs her and crawls back into the small tunnel.

"We need to do this right. You need to stay quiet or you can get us all killed," he says.

Amber just stares silently at Omani. Not only are her eyes glowing, but somehow her look is completely changed. She looks like a goddess with her changed hair, eyes, and skin. Her clothes are even different. They're an ivory color with flowing layers. Amber finds her quite mesmerizing to look at. Bryce slowly looks up, catching Omani's eye. The feeling of love is so intense that it's like his heart is beating with hers. Omani slowly looks away toward the sky. At the top of the building they see the shape of a pyramid. Omani begins to move in that direction as the demon gets back into the air, watching her every move. Omani gets to the top of the building by small stairs that appear as her feet approaches them. After she steps on them, they fade away so no one can follow. When she reaches the top it's like she has found a new world. She looks around and sees rays of colored light and auras that surround both living and spiritual beings that have never been seen before with the human eye. They glide across the sky, changing speed and location; a beautiful sight. Omani looks directly up above her head and sees a crystallized opaque continuous white light. When she looks straight ahead again she sees a bunch of evil entities coming straight for her at an extreme rate of speed. There are two ahead of the others diving directly at her. With no time to think, Omani reacts by placing both hands in front of her as a protective mechanism. Suddenly the rays of light rearrange themselves, and different colors form into one steady stream. As the stream approaches the evil entities they instantly become immobilized and disintegrate. When Omani realizes that nothing is attacking her, she removes her hands and finds that the entities are gone. She stands there bewildered, picking up her hands again and looking at a pretty ray of light close by. She notices that when she moves her fingers the rays of lights follow and change. She begins to use all of her fingers and notices even more changes. She finds it quite fascinating. Bryce and Amber are trying to see Omani but have difficulty. They see hand movements with no explanation.

"What is she doing?" Amber asks.

"It looks like she's holding something," Bryce replies, stumped.

Then Bryce sees the demonic entity coming from the side and going right for Omani.

"*Omani, watch out!*" he screams.

Just as Omani turns to look the entity knocks her down off the top off the building. Neither Bryce nor Amber can see her anymore. Amber gets up and starts looking around and sees nothing. She looks at Bryce, terrified.

"Where did she go? Where did it take her?" she asks.

Bryce gets up and starts running in the direction where Omani fell, hearing nothing. It's like Omani had fallen off the face of the planet. On the other side of the building they encounter a steep ledge with a cloud of dust at the bottom. Inside the dust Omani is getting up and the entity is laughing with a deep evil voice. It throws her around every time she tries to get up, trying to make her weak. After five times, it uses its thorns to keep her down as it approaches.

"This power has no use for you. It belongs to me. Give and you shall live," it says.

"It doesn't belong to you. It never has and never will!" she replies.

It starts to laugh again. Then it waves its hand in the air and a picture appears. It shows Bryce and Omani together walking down the aisle. It's a beautiful sight. But then it shows Bryce in a coffin and Omani alone with her powers.

"Look at what you can have. This power will only hinder you," it states.

Omani uses her legs to try to push it away. "Get away from me!" she screams.

It laughs again, pushing her to the ground. One of its thorns starts to squiggle at her, breaking free from its body. It holds her down, waiting for the thorn to enter her. She maneuvers herself free and gets away, but the demon becomes even angrier. A huge dark cloud forms in front of Omani. The demon uses its tail to push her into it. Bryce and Amber are standing on the ledge looking down as the dust cloud disappears only to be replaced by the dark cloud the entity has formed. The cloud swoops toward Omani quickly and engulfs her; the entity vanishes immediately following Omani's disappearance. Horrified, Bryce watches Omani disappear. The dark cloud is now gone, leaving no trace of either one.

"Now she's on its turf. What are we going to do?" Amber says, all upset and feeling like she just lost her sister forever.

Bryce thinks quietly to himself for a few minutes and then suddenly stands up.

"I need an evil portal!" he says.

"*What?*" Amber replies.

"That entity used a dark portal through the cloud to take her to wherever. I need one to follow them and help her," Bryce says.

"Are you crazy??!!! Talk about getting us killed," Amber replies.

"Look! I have to go in! If they get this power who knows what can happen. Besides that, if anything should happen to Omani I wouldn't be able to live with it. She's a part of my life now, and I can't imagine a day without her in it. Amber, she's my soul mate. If she dies, as far as I'm concerned so do I. I've been through enough tragedy in my life. I want no more if I can help it. Now I need you to be our rock and keep it together. Come on; I need your help," he says.

She gets up, wiping her eyes, and follows Bryce. They get the duffel bags and open them.

"What exactly are we doing?" Amber asks.

"We've always used these for good portals. Now it's time to attract a dark portal. Evil likes dark and gloomy. I have a special dark light flashlight that is supposed to attract evil, or so my aunt used to say. I guess it's time to find out if it works," he says.

"Your aunt wanted to attract evil?" Amber asks.

"No, it's how she cornered them. It's a long story," he says.

Bryce jumps down onto the next level of the structure, and Amber slowly follows. He turns on the light, slowly swinging it from side to side it to see what happens. Nothing occurs. But then they hear a strange noise. Amber turns around and sees a squiggly creature and screams. Bryce holds out his hand toward her to signal her to remain calm as he turns off the light. The figure backs up, thinking it's a trap. A dark shadowy light appears and begins to enter the portal by backing up.

"Stay strong. I'll be back," Bryce says.

"*But …*" Amber says as he leaps into the portal. The shadowy light disappears, but she doesn't hear a sound. She stands there, looking around and seeing nothing but desert and hearing nothing but the wind whirl around her. It's an eerie sound. She stands there, stunned and speechless.

Omani looks around after wiping her eyes, unfamiliar with the surroundings as she descends the winding tunnel. Arms reach out, trying to touch her. She hears voices but sees no faces anywhere. She keeps going down the dark tunnel, uncertain of what awaits. She knows that she must remain strong and ready to fight. Suddenly the tunnel comes to an abrupt end. On the other side she sees nothing but darkness. The feelings of doom and gloom are strong, like a powerful negative energy has just landed on top of her trying to take all the good out. The strange feeling is intense and uncomfortable, and with each breath the heaviness increases. There's no sign of life anywhere; just darkness. Omani tries to feel her way around to figure a way out but finds nothing. She places her hands in front of her to use the new power but no rays of light can be seen. All she can do is wait, but for what? She knows that something is lurking in the distance, but she can't see or hear it. She tries to remain calm but yet ready to fight at any given moment.

While she's trying to figure out the new surroundings, she senses a pair of angry red eyes starting to approach her slowly from behind. When the eyes get closer, not making a sound, a huge ball of light flashes directly in her eyes. It stings her eyes, causing her to start screaming and drop to a strange gritty ground that feels like it is constantly moving. The ball of light is so intense it blinds her and all she can see are flashes of white light. The red eyes get larger as they approach from behind, and she wipes her eyes, trying to stop the stinging. Suddenly she hears a deep growling sound and stops what she's doing and freezes. She doesn't even take a breath. After a few seconds she hears no further noises, so she slowly begins to turn around toward where the sound is coming from. As she tries to focus on whatever may be there, all she sees are flashes of white with a hint of red. The red eyes continue to get close to her and look her directly into her eyes with only an inch between them. It growls again, its nasty breath blowing on her hair. Omani tries to back up, but there's nowhere to go.

The nasty-looking entity has an inverted nose and four eyes, two in back and two in front. Its teeth are shaped like daggers, and its skin looks like it is always sloughing off, but it isn't. In fact, it is actually continually moving and changing positions. On its stomach people's faces that try to poke through but can't. Its scaly ears protrude, and its fingers are like sharp pitchforks. Its breath smells like five years of fermented garbage. Omani tries to crawl away but doesn't know where to go since she can't see. She feels around with her hands in front of her. The nasty entity touches her skin with its nails. She jumps back and straightens up. It starts to laugh intensely for a second but then instantly becomes quiet. Then it moves with lightning speed to a different position around her, but the smell of its breath gives it away. Omani holds her breath and reaches out, trying to push it away. She touches its stomach and hears peoples' screams. The entity pushes her to the ground, breathing heavily. The smell is overwhelming and gives her the dry heaves. She somehow gets one leg free and uses it for a footing to pull herself out. She knows that she has to be quick, so she does this in a matter of seconds and breaks free. She starts running but hits something and falls. The entity jumps on top of her, holding her face down.

Suddenly the environment changes as the entity screams and pushes on the slimy ever-changing walls. As Omani's vision slowly improves, she sees a cage appear and drop on top of her. Then two entities with beastly faces look armed, rugged, and dangerous. They hold strange-looking glowing sticks in their hands. Omani stands up and immediately touches the cage to try to get out. It shocks her, and she falls to the floor, drained of energy. The entity laughs as it moves quickly around. Then it goes into the cage as if the door didn't even exist and stands over her, laughing. She looks up, trying to catch her breath.

"Every time you touch the wall of that cage, your energy will be drained more. The guards that you see are going to help you with that.

You see, once you're weak enough nothing can stop me from entering you. And the best part is that no one can get in. That is, unless they want to die. Welcome to my world and my rules. Soon my world shall expand and all will know," it says, laughing again and then exiting quickly.

The guards move in with the sticks and start poking at Omani. The sticks sting like a bee, and every time they touch her, her eyes glow a little less. As they poke, Omani screams bloody murder. They force her up to touch the wall of the cage. Then she falls back down. The process is repeated a many more times. Then one of the guards enters the cage and picks Omani up and starts to feel her body. She tries to push it away, so it bites her while the other uses the stick. The dark entity begins to change form to a mist. She can see something forming out of the corner of her eye. She looks and is able to see its face for the first time. Omani is horrified by its appearance, but she is too weak to scream. The entity becomes a complete mist and enters the cage. The guards hold her down. She can barely stay awake. Just then, Bryce comes running through the end of the dark portal.

"Omani!! Omani, are you here?!" he says.

"Over here!" Omani says with little energy.

He knows that she is in trouble and starts running to where he heard her voice. But the mist begins to enter Omani's nose, and she starts to cough. She leans over, trying to vomit it out, but it is very strong. Bryce approaches the cage.

"No! Don't let it in, Omani! Fight it!!" he screams.

The mist is completely in her now. Bryce grabs hold of the bars of the cage and gets a nasty jolt, throwing him across the room. Smoke rises off of him, and he appears unconscious. Omani turns her head toward him. He sees her eyes turning red as she starts to growl and then laugh, and the noise turns from normal to sadistic. Then, he passes out. She stands up, raising her arms, and the cage disappears. She looks into the distance, strategizing.

CHAPTER 19

Iɴ ᴛʜᴇ ᴅᴇsᴇʀᴛ ᴛʜᴇ sky is blue with not a cloud to be found anywhere. Even though it is dry and hot, there's still wildlife out and about. Amber is sitting on the ground watching the wildlife while sifting through the duffel bag. She takes a deep breath, but then a strange feeling comes over her. She feels like there's a shadow hovering in the sky, so she looks up and sees the sky starting to change. She slowly gets up, shocked by the awesome changing appearance. The color is going from blue to an orange-red color and then to a hazy gray. The wildlife takes off for a hiding spot all at once. She knows that something is wrong and that it has something to do with her sister.

"*Omani!*" she says, horrified at what may be or has happened.

She instantly gets back down and fumbles through the duffel bag. When she looks back up she sees one specific cloud turning into the shape of a tornado. The winds start to pick up, so she grabs the bag and heads for cover. When she enters a small cave the winds come to an instant stop. It is eerily quiet, and she hears nothing, not even a bird. Amber tries to not even breathe because she has no idea what just happened. She slowly leans forward with the duffel bag extremely close to her. Taking a quick peek, she sees small holes opening up in the sky. She is scared but at the same time can't take her eyes off of everything going on around her. Suddenly small balls come out of the holes flying through the sky. They open up, and nasty-looking demons come out, screaming with angry revengeful cries. Their eyes are piercing and daunting to look at, so she turns away. The demons dive for and attack anything that moves, leaving nothing behind. They spread out and head off in different directions to cause havoc around the world.

Then a bigger cloud forms, and out of it appears Omani. She stretches as though just waking up from a long nap and lightly touches down on the ground. A nasty stench fills the air, making Amber gag. All living plants in the vicinity begin to wither and die.

"Amber," it calls out with her sister's voice, but not the way she would normally speak. It sounds very condescending and manipulative.

"What did they do to you?" Amber says very softly under her breath. Tears begin to fall down her face.

"Amber, I know you're here. I'm all right. You can come out. It's time for us to go home. We won," it says.

Omani walks around with those red eyes, looking for her sister. She has a smirking look of confidence and arrogance. Amber wipes her eyes, trying to keep from sobbing so she doesn't make any noise. She looks through the duffel bag, finding Grandma's glasses and holding them in her hand. She peeks around the corner and sees Omani, who looks okay. Then she puts the glasses up to her eyes. Suddenly Amber sees the horrible-looking demon and sits back, gasping from the shock.

"Oh Grandma, it would be so nice if you were here," Amber says.

Omani gets closer to where Amber is hiding and continues to call out her name. There's no sound or response, so Omani starts to walk in another direction. Then Amber's cell phone rings. She quickly tries to grab it to silence it. Omani immediately turns to where the sound is coming from and smiles. The phone rings a second time before Amber can get to it. She is so panicked that her fingers are sweaty. The phone slides to the ground and rings again. She picks it up and opens it, pushing a button for silence.

While all this is going on, Bryce is still lying on the ground in the cold dark place. His fingers begin to move slightly. After a few seconds, he lifts his head and opens his eyes and places his hands on his head, moaning. Then he places both hands on the wall to slowly guide himself up. It takes a few minutes for him to focus. Then it all comes back to him. He looks to where he last saw Omani. She is no longer there. Instead there's nothing but darkness. He hears screams of torture all around but sees nothing. As Bryce starts to walk, he staggers a little, seeing eyes that are on the slimy walls and move up it as though they are walking, watching him. They appear and disappear in seconds. Each time they reappear it is in a different spot. There are several different eyes changing positions, shapes, colors, and expressions. Bryce ignores them and keeps walking and looking for a portal. There's something in the near distance, so he approaches it only to discover that it's three different tunnels, all going in different directions. As he looks down one tunnel he can see flashes of fire and hear screams of torture. As Bryce starts to walk in another direction he slips and one of the tunnels pulls him in. He tries to grab something, but the tunnel's vacuum is very strong. He is pulled down the tunnel through a ring of fire. His foot gets caught in something that stops him from going any further. He looks to see how much further down the tunnel continues. Suddenly a flash of fire appears and he sees a person being tortured in the worst way. But before he can comprehend what's happening the light goes out. He hears something quickly coming up the tunnel, so he gets his footing and starts crawling fast. When he hits the top he quickly stands up part way partway and starts running. He looks back and sees a rotting arm descending out of the tunnel and then disappearing. Bryce takes a deep breath and starts looking for a way out. Then on the other wall he sees what appears to be a portal. He runs to it and is in it before he realizes what he's doing.

Suddenly he's outside in the desert, squinting his eyes in the brightness. In the distance he can see Omani with her back turned, focusing on something. He notices that she is different, and not in a good way. Bryce just stands there trying to decide what to do. Omani approaches Amber, who is trying to remain still and quiet as she hears her sister approaching. She puts her legs in a position to run, but then a feeling seems to come over Omani. She can sense Bryce and where he is located. She quickly turns around and looks directly at him. He is shocked by her swiftness as she starts to laugh and walks toward him.

"I see that my cage didn't quite get the job done. So allow me to finish it," she says.

Amber overhears the conversation.

"Bryce!" she whispers.

She jumps out of the cave with the canister open in one hand and the rods in the other. Tears are running down her face for what she is about to do. Omani turns around again, looking at her sister.

"And just what do you plan to do with that?" Omani asks.

"I know you're not my sister," Amber says.

She throws the dust in the air, forming a portal, and holds out the rods; Bryce comes running to her side. Omani starts to laugh, watching their frightened looks, and steps toward the portal, actually sticking her hand in it. Then she closes her hand inside and the portal fades away. Bryce and Amber look at each other in disbelief.

"That's for low-level demons. I believe it's my turn," she says.

She takes a deep breath and closes her eyes. Then she opens them and stretches out her arms. Bryce and Amber feel some trembling but don't see anything. They look at the ground, trying to figure out what's happening. The trembling intensifies, and suddenly something knocks them over. Amber isn't sure what to make of it. The back of Bryce's shirt is ripped open, and a long nasty scratch appears.

"*Bryce! Your back!*" Amber screams.

"Ow!!" he says as another scratch appears and starts to bleed.

Amber looks up, and Bryce watches as a scratch comes across her face.

"Come on!" he says, getting up and helping her stand.

Omani stands there laughing.

"Why can't we see them?" Amber asks.

"Because she's using her powers to prevent it," he says.

Amber stops for a second and puts on her grandmother's glasses. But just as she puts them on, something swipes them and they disappear.

"*Run!*" Bryce yells, pulling Amber in his direction.

In the near distance a huge group of black squiggly things start coming their way. Bryce stops for a second, looking around and realizing that they are surrounded.

"Come on!" Amber says.

"Just a minute," he replies.

Bryce closes his eyes.

"What are you doing? We need to go!" Amber says.

Bryce doesn't reply but just opens his eyes. Amber looks at him, terrified, as a black squiggly figure approaches them. Amber gets as close to Bryce as possible, screaming in fear. As the figure tries to get at Amber nothing happens.

"What happened?" she asks.

"I placed a protective shield around us. It's one of my powers. It can't get to us, for now anyway," he replies.

Amber lets go of him and takes a deep breath of relief. But she notices the squiggly things closing in and senses that there are the others that can't be seen. Omani notices the protective field and just smiles.

Her eyes begin to shine in a different color of red. Amber bumps Bryce's arm and points to her sister. Bryce notices what's going on.

"Is that Vuex in her eyes?" Amber asks.

"She is or it is using it. We don't have much time. We've got to figure something out," he replies, opening the duffel bags.

"Can't we do anything to help her?" Amber asks, watching her sister while trying to help Bryce.

"We need to get ourselves safe first and save Trent," he says, wiping the blood off his scratches.

Omani's eyes have a glow coming out of them that surrounds her body. It's as though some sort of transformation is taking place. Bryce and Amber rummage through the items from the duffel bag. Amber is trying to mix and match them, hoping something pops out at her as an instant solution. Bryce starts flipping through the documents, trying to find anything he may have missed.

"Where did she go?" Amber asks.

Bryce looks up and notices that Omani's not standing in the same spot.

"She's planning a surprise attack. Damn! There's nothing here to help us deal with this. There's nothing about Vuex and possession. Your grandma had to have something!" Bryce says.

He leans forward, reaching for something, and his tattoo and birthmark show on his abdomen.

"*Wait!* The birthmark. I mean tattoo or whatever," Amber says in excitement.

"What about it?" he replies.

"Did you ever figure out the reason for the symbol? I mean other than the connection to us?" she asks.

"It's a gateway … wait a minute! You're right. You can see it better than I can. Draw it in the dirt," he says, looking around.

Amber isn't sure about the reason for drawing it in the dirt but proceeds. She draws it large and as fast as possible.

"Okay, finished. Uh oh, trouble," Amber says, looking ahead.

Bryce turns his head and notices Omani, but with a twist. Her eyes are more piercing, like they are snapping. After a second he realizes what is happening.

"She's figured out how to cut through the shield. Her powers of Vuex are growing," he says, standing up and looking at the symbol in the dirt. Amber stands up too. Her grandma's necklace, which she always wears but usually keeps hidden, flops out of her shirt. The beautiful huge amber pendant sparkles in the sun. Bryce looks back and sees Omani approaching them but notices that she seems to be fixated on something. He follows Omani's eyes to the pendant.

"Take it off!" Bryce says, staring and pointing at the pendant.

"*No!* This is from Grandma," she replies, bewildered by the request.

"Not for me. Omani is fixated on it because evil is attracted to shiny pendants. My aunt told me that several times, but I never listened. Look, take it off or we die!" he says, pleading. Omani comes closer to the shield. Amber tries to get the pendant's lobster claw clasp open but struggles from the stress.

"I can't get it," she says.

The shield starts to glow a weird color and begins to thin. Bryce notices it and yanks the pendant off her neck, breaking the chain.

"I'll get you another chain," he says, placing the pendant in the center of the symbol in the dirt. Omani follows the pendant and stares at it inside the symbol as the ground in that area starts to shake. Bryce puts his arm out to push Amber back for safety. Omani focuses so hard that an intense beam of white light shines straight up to the sky for miles, so bright that it burns their eyes. Omani turns away from the burning and starts screaming. Suddenly the sky opens and a huge group of white things with wings come out.

"What's happening? Are those more demons?" Bryce asks.

"No ... they are ... *archangels!*" Amber says in shock and relief.

They come out at full force, armed and dangerous, and start attacking the demons in the sky and on the ground. They use special arrows and their touch to stop the demons, who come at them with no fear, only to be taken and never seen again. It is quite an awesome sight. The sky changes colors as the demons diminish in numbers. Omani starts screeching so loudly that it hurts Bryce and Amber's ears, and they fall to the ground, trying to block out the sound. Some of the archangels fall out of the sky and become motionless. While screaming, Omani uses the rays of light and her snapping eyes along with her hands to make a laser beam that streaks across the sky. Amber sees this happen and notices some of the archangels falling victim to the laser. She tears Bryce's shirt off his back and throws it with full force at

Omani. It lands on her head, covering her eyes. Bryce turns and looks at Amber, shocked.

"Well, it was either yours or mine," Amber says.

It gives the archangels just enough time to clear all the demons away, and they head back to where they came from. Bryce and Amber notice that the shield surrounding them has been broken. All the demons are gone except for one: Omani. She takes the shirt off of her face very angrily and lunges toward Bryce.

"Come on!" Amber says, pulling on Bryce to run.

"*No!* I've lost many people in my life. I'm not going to lose her too. Not if I can still save her," he says.

"But the demon has her," she says.

"Yes, but I know that there's a way to fight it. Nothing has worked, so I think it's time to use the oldest power in the book—love. She needs me, Amber, and you too. We can't leave her. Not now," he replies as he takes a step closer to the demon. Amber steps back, not sure what to say or do. She starts chewing on her nails, fearing the worst. The demon stomps its way to Bryce, staring directly into his eyes, but Bryce doesn't back down. Instead he stares right back at it, like it's a showdown. Omani takes her hand and touches his face with her pitchfork fingers, which scratch his skin, causing it to bleed. He lets the blood drip down.

"You can scare me all you want, but I'm not backing down. That's my girlfriend you took, and I want her back," he demands.

Omani screams. "She's not yours anymore," it says, laughing with an evil deep voice.

"*You can't have her!* She is my life. Without her I'm not complete. She's the best thing that has ever happened to me. I never knew what it was to love, but I do now. She is what makes my heart beat and my soul sing and brought back my desire to find happiness again after it was taken from me. I have lost so much in my life, but I will *not* lose her. *I love her!* You want something? Don't take her; take me! All she has is that power; I've got everything else. I'm what you're after," he says, taking another step closer.

Amber's mouth drops from the horror of hearing that statement, and she rushes to his side.

"Bryce!! You don't know what you're doing!" she says.

He pushes her aside without taking his eyes off the demon. The body the demon is in starts to shake, and its eyes start doing weird things. Amber steps back, not knowing what's going to happen. She reaches down and grabs the dust and rods just in case. Bryce takes another step closer, almost touching the demon.

"Let her go," he says, holding out one hand as though surrendering himself, with tears running down his face. The demon's body illuminates, and something jolts out of its eyes. It bursts out and goes up in the air, staring at Bryce and screaming. As it races toward him, it explodes and stuff goes everywhere. Omani is lying on the ground, unconscious. Bryce races to her side, and Amber wipes away her tears and runs to her sister.

"Omani," he says, holding her in his arms.

"Come on, sis. Don't let it win," Amber says.

There's no response. So Bryce tilts her head back, looking at her face. Then he slowly leans in and kisses her. She begins to move and wakes up.

"What happened?" she asks.

Bryce and Amber start to laugh.

"Oh, this headache," Omani replies, holding her forehead. Then she sits straight up. "The demon!!"

"Relax. It's gone!" Bryce says.

"What about Vuex?" she asks.

"I don't know; you tell me," he replies.

Omani stands up with the help of Bryce and looks around, taking in the environment. Then she sees a strange white floating figure coming their way. It stops in front of Omani. Bryce and Amber try to figure out what she is focused on. Omani looks a little more closely, and tears well up in her eyes.

"Grandma!" she says as her grandmother appears as a white silhouette.

Omani rushes to her side.

"Where?" Amber asks, trying to see her.

"She can't see you," Omani says.

"Use your powers so that she can," Grandma replies.

Omani focuses on their grandmother, and her eyes begin to glow. She lifts her hands, guiding the correct array around their grandma. Then rays of light take form and make her appear as though she is living.

"*Grandma!*" Amber shrieks.

They rush to their grandmother's side and hug her. The powers are strong enough to allow physical touch.

"I always knew you two were up to something. You take after me. You made me proud. Now that you know what you are, you must take care of your powers, for this is only the beginning. You're the guardians, and the future of balance is in your hands. Protect it. And to this young man I must say that you have a lot of courage, strength, and intense love. I am honored to know you. The sacrifice you made should teach us all a lesson. Come give Grandma a hug," she says.

Bryce goes up to her, and they hug tightly.

"I'm sorry we didn't listen to you more closely when we were younger," Omani says.

"Nonsense. You had every right to be skeptical. Being a guardian is not an easy job. Plus it shouldn't be taken lightly. Besides, you needed to figure things out on your own. Well, I must go," Grandma says.

"Must you? Can't you stay?" Amber asks.

"Oh, my dear one, I never left. Now that Omani has the power of Vuex I think we will be seeing each other a little more often. Oh, and I do believe that there's a boisterous gentleman you're looking for. Please take him away. The good thing is that he'll never remember anything I said to him. He'll be waking up in just a few minutes. Take care. Oh, and Bryce, it's okay," she says, winking at him. She kisses her granddaughters and then walks to the portal and fades as she goes through it.

"What did she mean by that?" Omani asks.

He shrugs his shoulders. "We can discuss that later. Right now, anyone want to go home?" he asks.

Omani and Amber agree and come together and walk toward Trent, who is waking up.

"What happened?" he asks.

"A field trip. Too bad you slept through it," Omani says.

"Oh," he replies, going along with the explanation. "So what did I miss?"

They all walk arm in arm, taking one leg and sweeping it in the same direction in the air all together and then bringing that leg down and doing the same with the other. They keep repeating the motion while heading to the car, talking and laughing.

CHAPTER 20

W HEN THE NEXT DAY arrives everything seems to be back to normal. The tension that has hovered over the sisters has been lifted; for now anyway. Omani is in the kitchen brewing coffee and peeling an orange. She is fully clothed and ready to start the day. She looks out the window, breathing a sigh of relief. It's like a new day and year that feel good with promises. A smile quietly comes across her face as she smells the aroma of coffee and turns around to get a cup of the fresh brew. Amber is finishing up in the shower. Bryce is coming down the stairs with his clothes all messed up. It's the "rolled out of bed" look. But he doesn't care; he feels like the conqueror of the world. Running his hands through his hair, he heads for the kitchen, yawning. He opens the door and immediately heads for Omani and hugs her tight and leans her back for a deep passionate kiss.

"Good morning. Wow, you were an animal last night. I think we should go to the desert more often," he says, kissing her again.

"*Grrrr!* What's stopping you?? By the way, thanks for being the man of my dreams. I can't wait to find out what's next," she says, whispering and grabbing his buttock. He chuckles, slowly walking away to get a coffee cup.

"Well, I was thinking that I would like to take you somewhere very special tonight," he says.

"The desert again?" she begins to say flirtatiously.

"Guess you'll have to wait and see. By the way, I want it to be just you and me," he replies.

"And just what time this evening will I find out?" she asks flirtatiously as she moves toward him.

"Let's make it around 6:00 PM, madam. And if you're late, you'll have to wait longer, if you know what I mean," he replies, bowing.

"It goes both ways, darling," she replies.

They both chuckle. Then Amber walks in fully clothed with wet hair and goes to the cupboard to get a cereal bar.

"Everybody feeling great today? I know I am. I'm so glad yesterday is done," Amber says, stretching. Bryce and Omani kiss and then try to resume the day's activities, coughing to clear their throats.

"Yeah, now if I can just find my phone," Omani says.

"You lost your phone?" Bryce asks.

"Yeah, we went to the desert, and that's the last time I saw it," she replies, taking a sip of coffee.

"Oh my gosh, the phone!!" Amber says, taking off running.

"I guess it was something I said," Omani says, turning to Bryce, who is admiring her with romantic eyes. She leans back against the counter, enjoying the flirtation, while taking another sip of coffee.

"Hey, babe, just make sure you dress up tonight," Bryce says, winking.

"Lingerie it is. That is, if you think you think you can handle it," she responds.

"Try me, baby," he says, winking at her again and leaving the kitchen. She looks out the window again, smiling and dreaming about the night to come. Then it's like a light suddenly goes on. Omani places her coffee cup down with a look of doom and concern in her eyes. Just then, the kitchen door opens and Amber walks in with her phone.

"I just realized that we never heard from those agents. We blew it!! What have I done??!! Oh my God, Amber, what are we going to do?" Omani says, distraught.

"Hold that thought. Where's Bryce?" Amber asks.

"He went back upstairs, I think. Didn't you hear me?"

Amber opens the kitchen door, yelling for him. Omani looks at her sister, puzzled by her reaction. Bryce comes running down the stairs half-clothed with only a robe on, thinking the worst.

"What's the matter?" he says, ready for another spirit fight.

"Nothing," Amber says, giggling. "You probably both don't remember, but yesterday when Omani was that thing the phone rang. I silenced it, but I never went back to check it. There's a message. I want you to listen," she replies.

Amber places the cell phone on the counter, using the speaker phone. There are a couple of messages from friends and one from her husband. Omani and Bryce look at each other, shrugging their shoulders and chuckling while hugging. Then a serious message comes on from one of the agents from the performance. Omani steps away from Bryce and closer to the phone, anxious to hear the message. Her hand begins to twitch from nerves.

"Hello, Amber. I tried to call your sister but got no response. So I will leave you a message in the hopes of receiving a call in return. I must say that I, as well as the others, was very impressed. I would like to discuss contract details. I will only be in town for two more days. So if I don't hear from you by then, I will assume that either you took another offer or changed your mind. All the best. Michelle."

After hearing that message the three of them start jumping up and down, screaming with great joy.

"*We did it!!*" Omani says, jumping up and down.

"I know; it's great! We've got to tell Trent and Gabe!" Amber says.

Suddenly Omani stops jumping up and down and goes over to the calendar on the wall.

"What's the matter?" Bryce asks.

"Well, if she called yesterday that means we only have today. Amber, call the other two and tell them to meet us downtown now!!" Omani says.

She rushes out of the kitchen, trying to locate her purse. They have come so far; this is a major mile marker in their lives. Bryce quickly goes to Omani, who seems to suddenly be going into a whirlwind. He turns her toward him, placing a finger on her lips. Then he holds her, giving her a sense of peace and security and whispering congratulations.

❦

A few hours later, everybody is at the house. Gabe brings his girlfriend and some champagne. Omani breaks out the glasses, and Gabe tries to open the bottle. He struggles and gets nowhere. Trent grabs it and tries it. He pulls a couple of times and gets nothing. So he places it between his legs and pulls even harder. The cork comes flying out and hits the ceiling and then the wall. Foam spurts out, spraying everyone, and they all laugh. Then Trent proceeds to fill all the glasses.

"How about a toast?" Gabe says.

Everybody stands in a circle, holding up their glasses.

"For all the hard work we did to get here. We have a lot more to go, but may major success await us. I'm so glad to have you all as my friends. Cheers!" Gabe says.

They all clink their glasses and take a drink. Trent holds up the contract and cheers loudly.

"We've got a lot of work ahead of us. But I know we can do it," Trent says.

The big celebration continues. Bryce pulls gently on Omani's arm, showing her the time on her wristwatch. She quietly looks up at the clock and notices that it's five thirty. Then she nods her head and approaches Amber quietly.

"Bryce and I are going to celebrate romantically. But you guys continue," she whispers. Amber nods. Omani heads upstairs to get ready. The laughing and carrying on seem to become more quiet. While they are getting ready all they can hear is silence. It's strange, especially since the cars are still there. Omani continues getting ready, but her curiosity about the silence is killing her. She heads down the stairs all dressed up, cautiously looking around. Did something bad happen? So many things start to race in her mind. There's no one around, that she can see anyway.

"Hey, guys," Omani begins to say while starting down the stairs. There's still no one. As she comes down further she sees Bryce standing at the base of the stairs.

"Where is everyone?" she asks.

"They went to get more champagne," he replies.

"But the cars ..."

He holds out his hand to gesture for her to come down the stairs. With hesitation she proceeds, wondering what's going on. He gently holds her hand and has her stand still. She begins to look around, thinking that something is definitely going on. Then she looks more closely at Bryce, noticing his threads for the evening.

"My, aren't you all dressed up and looking sexy? I vote to stay here," Omani says, flying into his arms. Bryce hugs her and then steps back. He wipes the palms of his hands on the nice dress pants and gazes into those mystified eyes. He coughs a few times to clear his throat and then gives her a strange smile. She stands back a little, wondering what's the matter. Then he nervously takes a deep breath and proceeds to get down on one knee. Omani's jaw drops.

"Omani, these past few weeks have made me realize how precious life is and how important is it not to not waste it. I've also learned that when something or someone special comes into your life you should hold onto it, for it may never come your way again. I have dated many women, but none like you. You've touched my heart in ways that no else ever can. And when I'm near you my soul sings. You make my life complete, and I can't imagine a day without you in it. Omani, you're the one for me. So would you do this man the honor of becoming my wife? Please. I need you forever," he says, opening a little box containing a diamond ring. Omani places her hands on her face in shock. She gasps for air while tears of joy run down her face and then falls to the floor, staring at the ring and gazing into his gorgeous eyes.

"Oh Bryce, I feel the same way. *Yes!!* I will marry you," she replies, jumping into his arms and hugging him so tight he can barely breathe. They both fall back onto the floor.

"Wait!! Wait!! I haven't put the ring on yet," he says, trying to breathe.

Omani comes up for a breath of air, holding out her right hand and shaking intensely. Bryce is able to take a slight peek through her shoulders.

"The other hand."

She laughs and takes her other hand from underneath him. Bryce places the ring on it, and they immediately begin kissing. As Omani is feeling their embrace, she hears the sound of a cough. She stops in the middle of the kiss, trying to look out of the corner of her eye. She sees a pair of feet standing there. She slowly takes her hands off Bryce, embarrassed, and they get up. There stands the rest of the band with big smiles on their faces quietly observing them. Amber races to her sister for a big hug. In the midst, Omani notices that the rest of the band is dressed up too.

"Wait. You knew?" Omani asks.

Amber nods. The rest of the group comes around and gives her a big hug. Amber has an especially beautiful long dress on. Both Gabe and Trent have tuxedos on. Trent comes over to give Bryce his jacket. He puts it on to complete the artistic-looking sensual tuxedo outfit. It has a distinguished classy look and an original rock 'n' roll appeal to it.

"What's going on?" Omani asks.

"Why don't you go to the back room over there and find out?" Amber says.

She walks to the room where the rock 'n' roll outfits and ensembles are kept. The door slowly opens; who knows what's on the other side? Omani looks around without entering. Nothing seems to be different. She looks back, and Amber gestures for her to go in; so in she goes, curious. All the outfits are in their cases as usual. She looks around, confused, and turns back to the door. Suddenly her face lights up. There in front of her is a white wedding dress with lavender flowers attached to it in certain places, making it look priceless. It has a beautiful empire neckline and looks like something a goddess would wear. It's covered with embroidery and has a flared hem and an open back. She sees shoes to match and a veil loaded with a variety of flowers. Omani starts to cry as Amber walks in, all smiles.

"How did you know?" Omani asks, startled.

"You remember a couple of years ago when we talked about weddings and what you would wear? You stated that you would probably never get married because there never seemed to be the right guy. But you proceeded to tell me about your dream outfit anyway. Well, I remembered," Amber says.

Omani hugs her sister tightly. Then Bryce comes into the room, looking at his watch.

"We need to go," he says.

"It's tonight?" she asks.

Amber nods. Omani can't believe what's happening. Tears start flowing as she looks back at the dress in utter shock.

"I'm getting married!!! I never thought this would ever happen to me! And it's to a man I love, and he's my dream. Please pinch me quick to make sure this is real!!!!!" she states. Amber pinches her sister hard enough to get a big ouch. Her sister closes the door to help her change. When she comes out of the room Bryce has already left with the other guys. Omani stands in front of the full-length mirror, amazed. Her sister smiles, putting on the finishing touches. She carefully places flowers in Omani's hair, making her glow. She can't help but stare in the mirror. Amber gestures to her sister to go to the front door to head out for the ceremony. As she exits the house she sees a large stretch limousine parked out front. Omani's jaw drops as she gasps for air. A sharply dressed man holds the door open, waiting to seat her. Amber picks up the train and guides her sister to the limo. The shock is so much to take in. Omani doesn't even know which end is up as she tries to keep it together. The next thing she knows, they are at a wedding chapel. Omani enters and immediately sees her parents. It's another unexpected surprise, and she's uncertain how to react. They look at her with extreme happiness. It's as though all the pain from before has now gone. They stand and stare at each other for a minute, not moving toward each other. Bryce notices what's going on while the guys and his semi-conservative parents try to keep him from looking at the bride. He's very worried and so breaks away and rushes to her rescue, trying not to look at her.

"I'll take care of this," Bryce says without looking at his soon-to-be wife.

Omani places her hand on him, squeezing his shoulder.

"No, I will. Look, since I got the power of Vuex I can see things in a way I never could before. I have so much more clarity now. I actually understand things so much better. I want to talk to them. But thanks," she says, walking away from Bryce and approaching her parents. They hug her and cry. Her father takes her by the hand, and the trio goes out of sight to the back of the church where the procession will begin.

"You look beautiful!" her mother says.

"Thanks, Mom. I'm so glad you both came. Did Amber tell you?" she asks.

"No, Bryce called us. He actually asked your father for your hand in marriage. It was quite touching," her mother says.

They hug with tears streaming down their faces. Omani then looks at her father, not knowing what to say or do. She sighs deeply, hoping that everything will come out right. They all know how volatile it has been. No one says anything.

"Look, I know things haven't been so great, but ..." Omani starts to say.

"The past is the past. Let's start anew. I believe I have a bride to walk down the aisle," her father says.

"Oh Dad! Thank you!" she says, crying while they all hug again.

Suddenly the music begins to play. Amber and Kyle go to the back of the church to check on the bride, and they all hug. Then Gabe, Trent, and Bryce's best friend from the previous band, Loras, come back. They all prepare by getting in position to walk down the aisle. Kyle takes the ladies' mother to be seated. Amber and Loras go down the aisle first. Then Gabe follows with his girlfriend and then Trent with a close friend of the sisters. Finally everybody stands waiting for the beautiful bride. Out she comes with her father, who gazes at her with pride. Tears fall down Amber's face when she sees them. Their father proceeds to walk Omani down the aisle, indeed a sight to see. Amber knows that the old grudge is now gone. The feeling of harmony and peace now fills the air. As Omani reaches the altar, Bryce squeezes and kisses her hand. It is very difficult for him to take his eyes off of her. But he proceeds to turn to her father and hug him. Afterward, the minister begins officiating the ceremony, and they finally get to the important part everybody has been anxiously waiting for.

"Do you, Bryce Freeport, take Omani Devantier Williams to be your wife?" the minister asks.

"I do. Omani, you're the love of my life, and I'm grateful to have found you. You complete me and have given me a new hope I never thought I would find," Bryce responds.

"Do you, Omani Devantier Williams, take Bryce Freeport as your loving husband?" the minister asks.

"I do. Bryce, not only are you the love of my life, but you're also my soul mate. My love is real and will be with you always. I look forward to spending every day with you. You changed my life forever, and it is a gift and an honor to have someone a special as you as my husband. I love you," she says.

"I now pronounce you husband and wife. You may kiss the bride," the minister says happily.

Bryce leans in, appearing to give a simple kiss. But instead he bends Omani back and kisses her deeply, getting a wow from the crowd. Then the couple hugs in a very intense and loving way. The crowd is taken aback. After the long beautiful hug, they wave to the crowd. In the distance, on the wall sitting on the shoulder of a porcelain angel inside the church, is their grandmother. She blows them a kiss, smiling, and then disappears.

The End